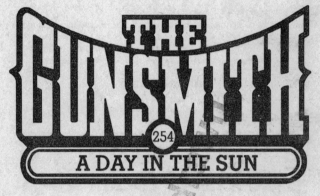

THE GUNSMITH

254

A DAY IN THE SUN

J. R. ROBERTS

D1454903

JOVE BOOKS, NEW YORK

This is a work of fiction. Names, characters, places, and incidents either are the product of the author's imagination or are used fictitiously, and any resemblance to actual persons, living or dead, business establishments, events, or locales is entirely coincidental.

A DAY IN THE SUN

A Jove Book / published by arrangement with
the author

PRINTING HISTORY
Jove edition / February 2003

Copyright © 2003 by Robert J. Randisi

Visit our website at
www.penguinputnam.com

ISBN: 0-515-13473-2

A JOVE BOOK®
Jove Books are published by The Berkley Publishing Group,
a division of Penguin Putnam Inc.,
375 Hudson Street, New York, New York 10014.
JOVE and the "J" design
are trademarks belonging to Penguin Putnam Inc.

PRINTED IN THE UNITED STATES OF AMERICA

10 9 8 7 6 5 4 3 2 1

ONE

Clint couldn't quite put his finger on it, but he just knew there was something peculiar about those men standing down on the street opposite his hotel window. They hadn't done much of anything since he'd arrived two days ago. They didn't even really talk to each other that much. There was just something about them that struck him as . . . peculiar.

Willett was a fairly decent sized town in New York near the foot of the Adirondacks. It was more than a village, but less than a city, and that was about all Clint could say about the place right off hand. He'd stopped there because it was at the end of his trail after a long day's ride, and he'd stayed there because he'd found a saloon that served good beer and was frequented by some old poker friends he hadn't seen in a while. There was a restaurant that served a fine steak, and of course there was Natalia.

A tall, voluptuous woman with long, raven-black hair and smooth, tanned skin, Natalia had an exotic Romanian accent and a body that was more than good enough to take Clint's mind away from heading back onto the trail for a few more days. She'd found him during a poker

1

game his first night in town and had been in his bed every night since. In fact, they'd been in bed every morning, as well as during a few lunches also.

With so much to do and someone like Natalia to do it with, Clint had kept pretty busy in Willett. That made it all the more surprising when he found himself noticing the men standing around across the street beneath his hotel window.

Standing there, bracing himself with his arm against the window's frame and staring down at the street below, Clint studied the men who seemed to be perfectly happy doing nothing . . . just as they had since he'd last seen them several hours ago.

"Clint, what is it you are doing?" came Natalia's thickly accented voice from the other side of the room. "Are you bored with me already?"

Clint smiled and shook his head, but didn't turn away from the window. "I'm a long way from bored."

"Then why don't you come back to bed with me? I want to get my legs around you one more time."

In the short time he'd known her, Clint had found that not only was Natalia a beautiful woman with natural talent in pleasuring a man, but she also didn't bother speaking with any subtlety whatsoever. When she wanted something, she asked for it. When she wanted Clint, she asked for him, too. She could be downright crude sometimes, but with that accent of hers, even the occasional profanity had some erotic ring to it.

Knowing full well the effect she had on a man, Natalia crawled on top of the bed. "I want you inside of me," she said with a pout. "Why do you keep me waiting?"

Every word she said had a way of rolling off her tongue. Her voice was a deep, throaty groan.

"Come here, Natalia," Clint said.

She reluctantly left the bed and stepped down onto the creaky floorboards. Wrapping her arms around him from behind, Natalia pressed herself against Clint's back and slid her leg up over his thigh.

Not only could Clint instantly feel the heat radiating from the woman's body, but he enjoyed the feel of her naked skin against him. As she ground against him, it became clear that she was not only completely naked, but also very anxious to pick up where they'd left off not too long ago.

"I want you," she whispered. "I don't want to wait."

Clint's first impulse was to turn around and let her strip him out of his clothes in the zealous, almost animal way she did when he kept her waiting more than a minute or two. But first, he moved his body so that he could hold her in his arms.

Natalia's skin had a dark, Spanish hue to it, but her facial features looked more European. She even tasted spicy when he pressed his lips against hers and kissed her deeply. Because they were so close to New York City, imported skin creams and fragrances were easier to come by, lending Natalia even more of an exotic charm.

All Clint had to do was open his mouth slightly while they were kissing and Natalia's tongue slid over his lips before darting between them. Her own lips were full and soft, and she moaned ever so slightly whenever Clint closed his teeth gently upon them. He did just that while letting his hands roam freely over her body, savoring the sensuous, uninhibited way Natalia sounded and moved while rubbing against his crotch.

It took all of Clint's resolve to pull away from the kiss and remember why he'd called her over to the window in the first place. "Do you see those men down there?" he asked while nodding toward the pair that had somehow caught his attention.

She seemed interested in nothing but him. Natalia's hands slipped over his chest and found their way between his legs, tugging at the waistband of his jeans. "You're the only man I care about now," she whispered.

"Just look for me, real quick."

With a sigh that seemed frustrated, yet more aroused because of it, she glanced out the window and down at the street. "Those two standing by the streetlight?"

"Yeah, those two. Have you ever seen them before?"

She'd already turned back to face him when she answered, "Maybe," in a voice that was more of an exhaled breath than a spoken word.

"Do they always stand there?"

This time, Natalia lifted her fingers to Clint's chin and forced him to look away from the window. "If you're so interested in them," she said, "I could leave and you could go down and introduce yourself."

She'd gotten Clint's pants open just enough to slip her hand inside and stroke the base of his stiffening cock. As she did this, Natalia stared into Clint's eyes, knowing exactly the effect she was having upon him.

Clint looked down at her and took in the sight of Natalia's body. Her breasts were large and supple, their dark nipples firm with excited anticipation. Her full hips were smooth to the touch and her legs were contoured with thin layers of muscle.

Standing completely naked and unashamed before him, Natalia stepped backward toward the bed, giving Clint a full view of what she wanted to give him. First, she ran one finger across her moist lips and then eased that same finger down between her breasts, over her stomach and down further to graze along the patch of dark hair between her legs.

She slowly turned around, displaying the round curve of her generous backside. Like a cat, she crawled back onto the bed and made her way until she could take hold of the headboard with both hands. When she turned to look at him over her shoulder, Natalia's dark brown eyes were smoldering like hot coals.

At this point, the only reason Clint wasn't on the bed with her was that he was enjoying the view so much right from where he was standing. He could feel his body aching for her, knowing how good it would feel to be inside of her and that she would let him indulge every desire he had. By the look in her eyes, she had some desires of her own, which Clint knew firsthand would be memorable in themselves.

No matter how peculiar those men looked, Clint was still a man himself. And since they still seemed to be happy standing across the street, watching silently as the rest of the town went by, Clint turned away from the window and made his way to the bedside.

As soon as his hands touched that smooth, dark, fragrant skin, Clint allowed himself to let those peculiar men stand on their own. Something in the back of his mind wouldn't let him forget about them completely, but at the moment he had other things to think about.

It didn't matter that their faces suddenly seemed vaguely familiar . . .

. . . or that the First Willett Bank was less than a block away.

TWO

Eight . . . nine . . . ten . . . eleven . . . twelve.

Ben Scott had been counting in his head for a couple days by now. When he'd first taken up his watch, he'd been counting the number of customers who walked through the doors to the little building on the corner of Second and Cedar Streets. It didn't take long to get a feel for the amount of business that the bank did in a day, which his scouts had said wasn't very much. Ben didn't have any reason to disagree with that assessment.

The next thing to count was the guards. Although the bank was at the end of a street, it was built so that it had a fair amount of space between it and the building next to it. There was no tight alley or rooftop within jumping distance, which ruled out two of Ben's favorite entry and exit options. That just left the doors and windows.

Being a bank in a town that wasn't exactly rich by any means, the building was watched by no more than three guards at a time. Again, Ben had known that much after listening to the scouts he'd sent into Willett several weeks ago. Three guards may have been a lot considering that the bank wasn't exactly stuffed to the rafters with money, but most of them seemed to be lawmen with nothing else to do who used sentry duty as a way to strut about with their rifles in hand.

That was the type of thing that Ben had learned after watching the place for himself a bit. That was also why he and the man beside him had ridden into town a day before the other five members of his gang arrived. While scouts were invaluable, there was no substitute for first-hand experience.

That type of experience was what had allowed Ben and his gang to knock over four other banks in the area, some of which were guarded twice as heavily as this one. He knew what he was doing and he knew what to look for. Counting might have been boring to most men in his gang, and impossible for some, but those numbers would make the difference once the bandannas were pulled over their faces and the guns came out of their holsters.

Standing in the spot he'd selected in front of a saloon and across the street from a hotel, Ben leaned against an awning post and watched the bank from the corner of his eye. Locals walked past him, going about their affairs without giving him or his partner more than a brief glance. Ben didn't look at them or away from them. Instead, he kept his expression neutral and his mind on his numbers.

"Twelve seconds," Ben muttered.

The man next to him snapped out of something that was close to a nap with his eyes open. He was a man of average build with bland, forgettable features. "What was that?"

Standing at just over six feet three inches, Ben wasn't as easy to overlook as his partner. But since he carried most of his two hundred eighty pounds in a soft mass around his belly, he found it easy to look harmless to most people who didn't know any better. When he wanted to, Ben could put on a wide smile full of crooked teeth, which was just so ugly that it was disarming.

Flashing that smile to a woman who walked past him,

Ben nodded and spoke in a subdued tone. "I said twelve seconds. That's how long it takes before one of them guards walking the perimeter crosses the front door. They've got themselves a nice little routine, so they're almost perfectly spaced."

Ben's partner had gone by just the name Ike so long that even the men he rode with had forgotten his last name. "So that means the door's clear for about . . . ten seconds?" Ike asked.

"Closer to six, but yeah."

Ike shifted on his feet. "When are the rest of the boys supposed to be getting into town?"

Taking a small brass pocket watch from a tattered vest that was held over his belly by a pair of buttons straining at their threads, Ben flicked the timepiece open and looked at the face. "Less than an hour now."

"If they're on time, that is."

"They'll be on time."

"They'd better be," Ike grunted. "Some of these folks is starting to look at us funny."

Ben laughed once and nudged his partner with one bulky elbow. "You're the funny-looking one that's attracting most of the attention."

"Oh yeah," Ike replied. "And you just look like every other fat-assed drunk that stumbles through these doors day and night. I still say we should find another spot to watch from. Some of these folks is looking at me, I tell ya."

"Don't get so nervous. We're not the only ones standing in front of this place. It's a saloon, for Christ's sake. It's made for people to stand around and do nothing. I think the owner's gonna be sad to see us go when we're done with this job."

Ike gnashed his teeth together and stuffed his hands into his pockets. "And when's that gonna be?"

"Soon, Ike. Real soon. Just shut up and relax. Why

don't you go get us something to drink while we wait."

Still grumbling under his breath, Ike turned on his heels and went into the saloon as he was told. Ben kept the easy smile on his face and nodded to a local man who passed by, just as he had the last couple days at this same time. Ben knew that he would pass the spot again in another couple of hours as well, which made him just as comfortable as it made Ike uneasy.

He knew that the locals were just about at the point where they were really starting to notice him as something more than just another stranger milling about in front of the saloon. Before long, they would start talking to him and then they would start to notice when he and Ike were missing from their spots.

But that didn't concern Ben too much since he knew he would be gone before he got on speaking terms with anyone besides his partner and the bartender. He prided himself on having a good feel for the way people acted and what was going through their heads. They would remember his face, but they had also stopped paying attention to him and Ike.

When on a job, Ben preferred it that way. He wanted to be seen as harmless, yet uninteresting. That way, when it was time to go to work, folks nearby wouldn't pay him any mind until it was too late. Ben knew better than to approach a bank when the locals were still wary of him. That only caused the guards to get jumpy and the whole job to get messier.

Bank jobs went smoothest when folks were confused and off their guard. Making them nervous ahead of time only made them skittish and quick to raise an alarm even before he and his gang got through the door. When that happened, the job wasn't impossible. It was just bloody as hell.

Ben didn't shy away from blood. In fact, some of his gang preferred to get their hands as dirty as possible. But they all agreed that banks in little towns could be taken down with next to no fuss at all so long as the job started out quiet.

Quiet meant blending in with the locals as much as possible so that the gang didn't attract any attention at all when they finally decided to make that walk up to the bank itself. The fewer people watching them, the more time they had to get in close and lock the doors without a hitch.

As a rule, Ben didn't like being watched. He preferred to be the one watching, which meant he didn't like the looks of that man who'd been staring at him through the hotel window for close to two days now. That one made him nervous.

As another rule, Ben hated people who made him nervous.

"Is he still there?" Ike asked as he came out of the saloon with two mugs of beer in his hands.

Ben smirked and shook his head. "Nah. He's gone. And just in time, too. It looks like the rest of the boys are here."

THREE

When Clint eased himself up onto the bed, Natalia grabbed hold of the headboard a little tighter and turned her head away from him. She arched her back just enough to display the smooth curve of her spine while letting her thick black hair flow down past her shoulder blades.

With the rich hues of the late afternoon sunlight pouring through the window and spilling across the room, her skin seemed to be the color of light caramel. Her scent drifted through the air, tempting Clint to move in closer without her having to say another word.

Everything else in Clint's mind was pushed to the side as he got close enough to slide his hands along the sides of her breasts and kiss her gently at the base of her neck. Clint allowed his instincts to take over and he took a little bite of her flesh, closing his teeth just enough to bring an excited squeal from Natalia's lips.

"Ooo, not too hard," she whispered.

"It's not my fault," Clint said between nibbles. "You're good enough to eat. And this perfume of yours makes you smell even sweeter."

She smiled and closed her eyes, savoring the feel of his mouth upon her skin. "It wasn't perfume. The bathwater

11

was scented. Maybe we can take a bath and you can try some for yourself."

"Later. I like it right where I am for now."

Natalia wriggled slightly, her hips grinding back and forth in a way that made Clint harder as he pressed against her. Once she felt his cock fully erect against her buttocks, she let go of the headboard and pressed the side of her face against a pillow, raising her backside up even higher.

After allowing himself to take in the sight of her for a moment or two, Clint ran the palms of his hands over her breasts, reaching out to tease her nipples between thumb and forefinger. She made a sound that resembled a satisfied purr, which turned into a throaty groan as he moved his hands down along her body.

Straightening up as he went, Clint slid his hands farther toward her waist until he could massage the firm roundness of her ample backside. He wanted more than anything to get inside of her, especially when he could just make out the wet lips between her thighs.

Just to torture him further, Natalia spread her legs wider while lifting her buttocks a little higher.

Clint might have enjoyed the anticipation, but he could only take so much. He could feel his pulse throbbing throughout his entire body, growing to a heat that started to border on pain the longer he kept holding himself back. Finally, he gave in and fit the head of his penis into the soft, moist spot between her legs.

Clint took hold of Natalia's hips with both hands and pulled her closer while thrusting forward with his hips. He slid inside of her easily, the torture ending while the fire inside of him blazed even higher.

Feeling him thrust inside of her, Natalia clenched her eyes shut and clutched the pillow tightly against herself. She'd been aching for this moment to arrive, and now that it was here, she couldn't hold back the moans of ecstasy that welled up within her. After the first couple of thrusts, Natalia found Clint's rhythm and started rocking her body in a way to complement it.

Clint's hands were clamped around her hips, guiding her motion and allowing him to pound into her with greater force. When their bodies met, they both let out a satisfied moan. Entering her from behind, Clint was able to thrust deeply into her, hitting all the spots that caused Natalia's cries to grow louder with every second until they filled the room.

Suddenly, Natalia lifted her face from the mattress and opened her mouth as if she was about to scream. No sound came out, however, as she looked over her shoulder and into Clint's eyes.

She didn't need to say a word for Clint to know what to do. He slid inside of her one more time and stopped with his shaft buried within her moist folds. After pulling out slightly, he grabbed her hips and drove into her as deeply as he could, driving Natalia over the brink and headlong into a screaming orgasm.

Listening to her as she cried out in the midst of her passion, Clint felt his own body responding to her climax. But he managed to keep himself under control just long enough to ride out Natalia's writhing until she was covered in sweat and breathing heavily into the pillow.

Clint pulled out of her and took hold of Natalia's legs to maneuver her onto her side. Feeling his hands controlling her, Natalia looked at him with renewed vigor, her eyes wide with excitement.

"You're not done with me yet?" she asked with a hopeful expression on her flushed face.

"Not by a long shot."

And with that, Clint straddled one of Natalia's legs while setting her other one up on his shoulder. From there, he guided his penis over her thighs, teasing the lips of her pussy until she was begging for him to enter her once again.

Clint was only too glad to do so, and when he was inside, he felt a new set of sensations as he thrust in and out from this new angle. From there, he could also get a better look at Natalia's breasts as her chest heaved with every heavy, passionate breath. She rubbed her own large, dark nipples when Clint took hold of her raised leg, groaning loudly as he pumped his hips between her thighs.

Using every last bit of strength he could muster, Clint held on to Natalia's body and thrust into her one last time. He exploded within her in a rush that felt so good it set the room to spinning around his ears.

Feeling the muscles in Natalia's body clenching around him, Clint reached down and ran his fingers over her clitoris until he heard her breath catch in her throat. It wasn't long before Natalia was thrashing against him and crying out breathlessly as a second orgasm swept through her body.

"Oh my god," she sighed while slumping down onto the pillow.

Clint moved so he could lay down next to her, unable to do much of anything else once his body hit the mattress. "You took the words right from my mouth."

FOUR

After a few minutes had gone by, Clint found some energy creeping back into his muscles. It wasn't easy, but he managed to sit upright and swing his feet over the side of the bed, stretching his back before standing up.

Although she looked as if she'd been asleep, Natalia rolled on to her stomach and reached out for him. "Clint, why do you want to go?" she asked sleepily.

"I don't want to go. Just stretching my legs, that's all."

Holding on to him tightly by the wrist, she pouted. "If you want to stretch, you can stretch right here. I can stretch on top of you."

The woman's accent caused her to roll all her r's and add a sultry breath to the end of her sentences. English was plainly her second language, but she spoke it in such a way that almost had a hypnotizing effect on any man who heard it.

"Normally, I'd say you could do anything you wanted on top of me," Clint said. "But if I don't take a minute here, I might not make it off that bed."

"Would that be so bad?"

Clint turned to look at her over his shoulder. Natalia was reclining on her side with one hand resting on her hip and the other sliding along his forearm. Her skin was damp with the perspiration they'd both worked up together. Not only did she not make the first attempt to cover her naked body, but she seemed to take more pleasure from the fact that Clint wasn't taking his eyes off of her. She writhed on the bed and smiled invitingly, touching herself wherever he happened to be looking.

Sliding his fingers through her coal-black hair, Clint pulled her closer and kissed her on the lips. He broke off before she took him to the point of no return, however, and got to his feet.

"If I didn't know any better," he said, "I'd think you were trying to kill me."

Natalia made a sound that resembled a pouting moan. Even though his back was to her, Clint could almost picture her sticking her lower lip out in that way that all women seemed to instinctually know. If it wasn't instinct, every female must be taught the expression by her mother as a way to wrap men around her little finger whenever she wanted to get her way.

While Clint found the pout undeniably sexy, he was old enough to break free of its power to bend the male will. But just to be sure, he was certain not to look at Natalia while she was naked *and* working her persuasive powers over him. There was something strange going on outside that he wanted to check on before losing track of time in Natalia's arms yet again.

After pulling on his jeans, Clint went to the window and looked outside. The first thing he noticed was that the two men who'd been nailed to their spots in front of the saloon were no longer there. His curiosity piqued, Clint scanned the street and quickly picked out the several other figures hurrying down it as if someone had set their britches on fire.

"Clint . . . I want you to lay with me," Natalia said.

"Come away from that window . . . unless you'd rather look there than at me."

"Something's going on out there," Clint said.

He looked in the opposite direction from that the people were running in, just as a distant scream drifted through the air. Clint's window was closed, but the glass was loose enough in its frame for him to hear the woman's voice as she cried out. And the gunshot that followed was even easier for his ears to pick up.

Clint felt his blood pump quicker through his veins and his strength flow back into him when he heard that shot. Throwing open the window, he leaned outside and looked down the street to find that the people he'd seen had been running away from the bank. Clint would have bet every penny he was worth that the gunshots had come from there as well.

On top of that, he was getting a sneaking suspicion he knew where he might find those two that had been watching the street for the last couple of days.

"What are you doing?" Natalia asked. "What's so wrong?"

Clint was already pulling the rest of his clothes on and cinching his gun belt around his waist by the time both questions came out of her mouth. A constant flow of motion, he darted about the room collecting what he needed and was opening the door in a matter of seconds.

"Just stay here," he answered before stepping into the hall. "There's trouble outside."

Natalia started to say something, but Clint couldn't make out what it was through the closed door.

FIVE

Watching the way Ben moved, not one of the locals standing outside the bank would have guessed that he was the same fat man who'd been taking up space in front of the saloon for the last few days. Bolting out from the bank, he and the rest of his men flew over the wooden planks of the boardwalk as though their feet didn't even touch down. They all wore dirty bandannas wrapped around the lower half of their faces as well as long coats to conceal the weapons they were carrying.

Ben was the first one out. He hit the street and glanced around to make sure that the law wasn't about to jump down his throat. Although there wasn't a badge in sight, there were plenty of locals who were either curious or brave enough to try and stop the robbers. The valor in their hearts quickly faded when Ben fired a shot or two over their heads.

"Come on, let's go!" he shouted to the men behind him.

The five who'd just ridden into town came out next. Two of them hefted saddlebags over their shoulders that hadn't been full when they'd gone in. The two with the bags each carried a shotgun, while the others had a pistol in each fist. Last through the door was Ike. He was still shouting instructions to the tellers and customers inside as he backed out of the bank.

"Stay down!" Ike shouted through the bandanna which made his voice sound slightly muffled and deeper. "Nobody move a goddamn muscle!"

Just then, one of the guards came running around the corner of the building. He was one of the younger ones and hadn't been on the job long enough to learn that caution served a man better than guts in certain situations. He came barreling toward the robbers with his rifle held in both hands.

"I got him," Ben said to the men behind him as he turned toward the approaching rifleman.

The guard barely got a look at the big man before Ben's pistol cracked once and sent a piece of hot lead through the air. Pain spiked through the guard's chest for a moment and he was knocked backward off his feet.

As he fell, the younger man's vision started to blur and all the sounds became a garbled mess. He didn't feel his back slam against the ground, but he could feel every drop of blood that leaked from the hole in his chest and back as his heart pumped its final beats.

All the robbers were out of the bank by now, and Ben was already heading for the horses tied up nearby. He shifted his eyes back and forth over the crowd that had been passing by when they'd busted out, satisfied for the moment since most of the onlookers were lying on the ground.

One of the men with the saddlebags ran up to a horse and tossed his cargo over the animal's back. "You see any law?" he asked the fat man who was covering him.

Ben shook his head. "Not yet, but they're coming. And there's one more guard around here somewhere."

The second man holding a saddlebag was loading up his own horse as he said, "That one's probably shitting his britches right about now."

Although the final two robbers were at their horses by now, Ike was still backing slowly away from the bank. Ben turned to him and shouted, "We made it, now let's get the hell out of here!"

Ike had just turned away from the bank when a shot blasted from inside, shattering the large painted window facing the street. Already spinning back around to look toward the bank, Ike's shoulder left a thin, bloody trail in the air.

Instinctually, Ike ducked down low as he opened fire on the bank. He did so confident that he wouldn't be the only one sending lead into the building. He wasn't disappointed, as Ben and one of the others squeezed off a few rounds which blasted out the rest of the window and punched holes through the bank's door and wall.

The burst of gunfire sounded like a thunderstorm erupting in the middle of town. It was short, yet furious, leaving everyone but the robbers shaken right down to the core. Ben and the rest of his men took advantage of the panic they'd created and got ready for the last part of their job.

Both men with the saddlebags climbed onto their mounts while Ben untied the horses. Ike jogged up to the rest of his partners, and it was only then that he noticed the pain in his arm and the blood on his shirt.

"Shit," Ike grunted. "I caught one."

None of the men on horseback seemed to care one bit about what Ike had said. They were too busy reining in their horses and pointing them in the right direction. Not even Ben seemed to care too much until after he'd smacked the two horses on their rumps and started them galloping away with their important baggage.

SIX

Ben finally turned to Ike and quickly looked him over. "It's not much. I'll take care of it, but we got to get out of here first."

Nodding, Ike climbed onto one of the remaining horses.

"Stop right where you are!"

The voice didn't come from the bank. Instead, it came from farther down the street, where two men were running toward the robbers' position. When they saw the masked men turn to face them, they dropped closer to the ground and sought cover.

"That's the sheriff," Ike said as he prepared to ride. "I recognize him."

By this time, each of the robbers had either climbed atop one of the horses that had just been ridden into town or one of the two that Ben had tied up in that same spot so they'd be there when this moment arrived. Ben snapped back the hammer of his pistol and raised the gun to eye level, just as he spotted motion from the corner of his eye.

This time, what he saw did come from the bank. Or rather, it came from the side of the building opposite from where the first guard had come running. Cursing under his breath, Ben started to take aim at what he thought for certain was the second guard. But before he could draw a bead on the man, a shot rang out and a bullet whipped through the air toward the robbers.

The familiar hissing sound ended with a wet slap of lead meeting flesh, followed by a pained groan. Ben had spotted the guard peeking from behind the bank and was sighting down his barrel to take a shot when Ike's voice drifted through his ears.

"Dammit," Ike grunted. "I don't think I'll . . ."

The rest of what he was going to say drifted off into a wheezing breath. Moments later, Ike toppled from the saddle and dropped in a heap on the ground. Ben only had to take a quick look at the awkward way his partner had landed to know that he wasn't going to be getting up. Ike's body looked like a doll that had been dumped onto its head, while the rest of his body folded up like an accordion on impact.

Once again, the robbers fired their guns in a continuous barrage. This time, the storm lasted longer and set the locals who'd been laying nearby into motion. Once they got to their feet, the onlookers started running down the street, putting as much distance between themselves and the bank as possible.

Some of the women started screaming, while the men shouted to try and be heard over them.

The sheriff and deputy that had just arrived opened fire as well, drawing some of the robbers' lead in their direction.

Ben cursed loudly as both of the men with the saddlebags put the spurs to their horses and took off in different directions. In their panic, one of those men rode toward the street where the sheriff was and caught a slug in the upper chest.

Reeling back as though he'd been hit with a two-by-four, that robber was knocked sideways off his horse and landed with a thud on the ground.

Once the blood of their own stained the dirt, Ben could feel the rest of his men yearning to break loose. Instead, they kept their heads and focused their fire to cover their prearranged getaway.

Seeing this, Ben smiled and added his fire to the mix. They were going to make it out of there after all.

Without missing a beat, another of the robbers holstered one of his two pistols and jumped into the saddle that had just been vacated. "I'll take the money out of here," he said, while squeezing off a couple shots toward the lawmen.

"I'll cover you and we can meet up where we agreed," Ben replied. "I can only see two law dogs down there and this asshole guard."

Just as those words came out of Ben's mouth, he spotted the second bank guard running toward him. He'd only turned his back on the building for a moment, but the guard had seized that moment so he could rush toward the robbers for an easier shot.

Even as he pulled back on his hammer to get ready to fire, Ben knew that he wasn't going to be able to get a shot off before the guard had a chance to do the same. He braced himself for the worst as he clenched his teeth and worked the hammer with his thumb.

The guard looked several years older than the first one who'd come running. His eyes were fixed on Ben as though he knew the fat man was the robbers' leader. The rifle in the guard's hands was already levered and ready to go as he brought it up and tightened his finger around the trigger.

A shot blasted through the air. Although there were plenty of guns going off at that particular time, this shot caught Ben's attention because it came from his immediate vicinity. Also, since he'd been watching the guard, he'd been readying himself for the shot that was surely on its way. Ben was also preparing himself for the pain that always came along with getting chewed apart by a bullet.

But there was no pain. Ben wasn't even knocked back a step. Instead, he realized quickly that he wasn't even hit. More than that, the shot hadn't come from the guard.

Ben blinked once and let out the breath he'd been holding. That's when he noticed that the guard's chest was spread open like an animal that had been half-eaten by wolves. The guard stopped in his tracks, let out a gasping breath and fell over. Only then did his rifle go off, sending its round into the dirt several feet short of its intended target.

Ben spun around toward the source of that last shot. He looked down and saw that the robber who'd been knocked off his horse wasn't quite dead. He held his shotgun in one hand, still pointing at the spot where the guard had been before the other man hit the dirt.

Although he started to help his partner to his feet, Ben stopped when he saw the shotgunner's eyes glaze over as the last little bit of life drained out of him.

"We've got them laws pinned down," one of the remaining robbers shouted.

Ben turned away from the dead shotgunner and pulled himself onto his horse. "All right, then. Let's skin out of here!"

Snapping the reins across his horse's neck, Ben got the animal running full speed. He steered in the direction where the other shotgunner had gone, knowing full well that the rest of his men were behind him. In a matter of seconds, they'd ridden far enough down the street to get out of the sheriff's line of fire.

It was going to be an easy ride from there.

SEVEN

Clint burst from the hotel and hit the street running. All he had to do was follow the sounds of chaos to know which way to turn once he was out the front door. There were already people charging toward him in a panicked stampede of waving arms and excited voices.

Gunfire crackled down the block, and once Clint pushed through a thick group of frenzied locals, he could see the black smoke hanging in the air near the bank. As he watched, more shots were fired and a single horse took off at a full gallop coming toward him.

Before Clint could get much of a look at the horse or its rider, it turned sharply and disappeared in a wide space between two buildings. Clint didn't really need much more of a look than that to let him know that whoever was on that horse wasn't exactly working to help the situation.

Rather than try to catch up with the speeding horse or take time to collect Eclipse from the livery, Clint kept moving toward the bank. There were still others in front of that building who seemed pretty anxious to get on horses of their own. Besides that, once Clint was a little farther down the street, he could make out the masks on the faces of those men.

Clint's senses rushed to take in everything around him, making sure that he wasn't about to run headlong into the barrel of a desperate man's gun. He was also searching for anyone that might be hurt or in immediate need of help. All he could see, however, was the men on horseback. They were shooting down the other street at the bank's intersection when one of them fired a shotgun.

Although he couldn't see much between the rearing horses and gritty smoke, Clint could tell that someone among the horsemen took the brunt of that blast.

"Dammit," Clint snarled under his breath as he forced his legs to move faster.

He was finally only a few storefronts away from the bank when Clint got a good look at one of the horsemen. The man's face was covered, but his build was unmistakable. Seeing that rotund frame triggered all the suspicions that had been running through Clint's mind over the last couple days, eliciting another, more potent curse from the back of Clint's throat.

Accusations began to fly within Clint's mind, all of which were aimed at himself. He should have paid more attention to his instincts. He should have approached those two that had been watching that bank. He should have told the law about them.

All Clint had to see was the panicked face of another local woman running for her life for him to realize what he really had to do. He had to put everything else aside and make sure that these men didn't just ride out of town without anything standing in their way.

Once that was firmly in mind, Clint shut out of his mind everything else that was going on so he could focus solely on those horsemen. His thoughts flowed more smoothly that way, which was exactly how he normally worked when things got fast and furious.

His instincts allowed him to look at things as though they'd slowed down around him, giving him the advantage over anyone who was fraying around the edges. The first thing he saw was that it was too late to meet up with the horsemen near the bank. All of the masked men were already in their saddles and starting to ride away. Trying to catch up to them now would be futile. That left him only two other options.

First, he could draw his gun and pick them out of their saddles before they made it another ten feet. If he was only concerned with putting them down, that would have been easy enough. But since he wasn't the type to jump into killing as his first answer, Clint decided to take his second option.

Less than two seconds had gone by since he'd first started thinking about what he should do. And once Clint had arrived at his conclusion, his body took over and he launched himself into action without even considering looking back.

Still running at full speed, Clint changed his direction by about ninety degrees, heading for the boardwalk to his left rather than the bank which was straight ahead. He dodged the locals who were either running in the opposite direction or standing still not knowing what to do next. His boots flew over the wooden slats, carrying him around the corner just as the next horseman was turning down that street.

If that rider had chosen to go another direction, he might have left Clint with only one option. But as it was, he followed in the previous horseman's steps, just as Clint knew he would.

Criminals liked their routines. Bank robbers lived by them. After dealing with his fair share of the bad element, Clint used that knowledge to his advantage and put himself in the right spot at the right time.

Without breaking stride, Clint looked at the edge of the

boardwalk to see if there was anything for him to work with. He had less than a second to think of some way to press his advantage before the robber simply passed him by and went along his merry way.

The only thing that caught Clint's attention was the railing that ran along the length of the boardwalk. It was made to keep folks from falling into the street, so it seemed sturdy enough. At least Clint prayed it was sturdy enough as he kicked in another burst of speed, launched himself up with one step and landed with his other foot on top of the railing.

For a moment, he felt himself teetering precariously in midair. His balance shifted as the railing wobbled beneath his boot, but by the time he was about to fall off his uncertain perch, Clint launched himself out into the street just as the horseman thundered by.

Holding both arms open, Clint braced himself for impact. The first thing he felt was a blunt pain filling his entire upper body as his shoulder made contact with the passing horseman's midsection. But rather than slam against the other man and topple onto the ground, he took the horseman with him and both of them sailed through the air.

Their landing was anything but pretty. Clint had one arm wrapped around the horseman's waist. His tackle had plucked the masked man off his horse's back and deposited him halfway into a water trough on the side of the street. Clint slid forward and managed to tuck his head in tight, turning what could have been a painful landing into an almost-impressive roll.

The horse didn't seem to notice right away that it no longer had a rider and kept right on running down the street.

As amazed at himself as he was, Clint didn't allow himself any time to celebrate. There were still four more horsemen closing in on him and his element of surprise had run clean out.

EIGHT

One minute ago, the getaway had been under control. And in the space of a few seconds, it had dropped straight back to hell.

Ben had been watching everything in a calculating, almost detached kind of way. Even as he fought and ran right alongside his men, he viewed things as they happened as though he was merely one of the countless faces looking on from the outside.

He led by example and he pointed the others in the right direction. He'd even gotten away from the law and managed to pull everyone back on track with all the money in tow. But then, he'd also seen something fly from out of nowhere to knock one of his men off his horse and dump him in a heap on the ground. Even worse was the fact that that damn horse was still running away.

"Catch that damn nag!" Ben yelled to the man riding beside him. "It's got some of the money."

With that said, Ben turned his full attention back to what was happening directly in front of him. His horse was about to ride right past the spot where the other robber had just been taken down, when Ben noticed some-

29

thing that caused him to nearly fall out of the saddle himself.

He recognized the face of the man who'd thrown himself through the air like some kind of damn crazed bird. It was the one face he'd been confident that he wouldn't have to look at for a good, long time. It was the one face that he was afraid might just mess this entire day up beyond all repair.

"Jesus Christ," Ben snarled beneath the bandanna that was stretched across his face. "It's Adams." Raising his voice so he could be heard by the men who'd fallen in behind him, Ben said, "It's Clint Adams! One of you go after that money and the rest of you come with me."

Confident that he still held authority over his men, Ben pulled on his reins and brought his horse to a stop. One of the others thundered past, but the remaining two stayed with him. Ben looked down from the saddle as Clint was scrambling to his feet.

"Gun him down!" Ben ordered.

He didn't have to say another word before the air was once again filled with lead. Unfortunately, the first two shots hadn't come from him or either of his men who'd stayed behind. Instead, they came from the Colt that had damn near materialized in Clint's hand.

Ben hadn't seen the other man draw.

He hadn't even seen him move toward his holster.

One second Clint had been straightening up, and then next he was already firing off his second shot.

All three robbers had already been shifting their aim to sight in on their new target. Even though they still held their guns in hand and were a heartbeat away from firing, they all felt as if they'd been caught with their pants down as the lead started to fly around them.

Taking the first rider down with his flying tackle was a spur-of-the-moment decision that Clint didn't have time to regret. Since that man was barely moving and groaning with fading consciousness, Clint figured he'd accomplished what he'd set out to do. He didn't find himself in the best of positions afterward, but that was a problem to be solved later.

Actually . . . it had been later a couple seconds ago and he was now in need of that solution.

Clint heard the command to fire given by the fat man, but pushed that to the back of his mind. What concerned him more at the moment was that one of the riders had kept on going and was about to get away. Figuring he'd be damned if any of those men were going to get away after he'd nearly killed himself with that fool stunt, Clint drew his Colt and fired a round at the escaping rider before he got out of range.

That first shot whipped through the air and closed in on its mark. Since the target was a horse running at full speed over uneven road, the bullet didn't hit the exact spot Clint had wanted to put it, but it got close enough to achieve the desired effect.

The chunk of hot lead burned a path close enough to the horse's flank to take a painful bite from its hide, but didn't do anything more than give it a deep scratch. It also gave the horse a shock, causing it to stop what it was doing, rear up on its hind legs and pump its front legs into the air.

The robber sitting in the saddle had barely heard the shot over the thundering of hooves and was taken completely by surprise when the horse decided to throw its tantrum. He instinctively grabbed onto the reins, but wasn't able to hold on tight enough to keep from being thrown off the animal's back and onto the ground in a painful heap.

Clint didn't have the luxury to watch if his first shot hit or not. Instead, he was shifting his sights toward the men trying to kill him, and when the Colt spat out its second round, it sent the bullet into the rider who'd been unlucky enough to get both his pistols drawn. The only reason that robber wasn't killed was that Clint didn't want him to die and had aimed for something less vital than heart or head.

So far, Clint knew he'd gotten the drop on the robbers. He'd even managed to retain that drop after they'd spotted him and come circling back to finish him off. They didn't seem spooked by his speed, however, and were a long ways away from turning themselves in. Just to be sure, however, Clint decided to give them a chance to use their heads.

"You're not getting out of here," Clint said as he got to his feet and covered the men in front of him with his Colt.

Ben and the pair beside him had had enough time to draw their weapons. Both of the fat man's partners held a pistol in each fist, which filled them with just enough confidence to stand their ground even as the law was closing in behind them.

"You should've done yourself a favor and stayed locked up with that bitch I sent to keep you busy," Ben said.

Clint's eyes narrowed and he fixed the fat man with a stare that would have sent plenty of men heading for the next train out of town. "What did you say?" he asked.

"You heard me. That sweet thing was supposed to keep your hands full, but I see she wasn't sweet enough to do that. Too bad, because now we're gonna have to take time out to execute you."

NINE

For the first time in what felt like an eternity, the street seemed to be totally quiet. Despite the fact that all of the men facing each other already had their weapons drawn, Clint was outnumbered three to one until the sheriff and his men got close enough to lend their support. Four to one if the robber who'd been thrown from his horse wasn't knocked unconscious.

Clint looked from one face to another, wondering which of them would attack first. None of them seemed too anxious to take the lead in this particular instance. There was a good and simple explanation for that.

"So you know who I am?" Clint asked.

Ben nodded once. "I recognized you coming in and out of that hotel. That don't mean we're gonna run scared."

"That was your first mistake."

"Well, I don't plan on making another." And with that, Ben started to lift his gun and take aim.

The move was a well-practiced fake, designed to draw Clint's attention for the split second that one of the other robbers needed to get the drop on him. It would have been a boost to Clint's ego if he could have said that the fake

33

didn't work, but that would have also been an outright lie.

It worked well enough and did exactly what it had been designed to do. Clint had started to shift his aim toward Ben when he noticed that the fat man was instead going to try and dive to one side while the other men around him closed in for the kill.

Clint saw what was happening and knew he'd fallen into the little trap. Fortunately for him, he was fast enough to change directions and shift his aim yet again before either of the robbers could take his shot. That much, at least, was enough to make Clint feel better for letting himself get suckered in the first place.

The moment that Clint hesitated was barely enough to be seen by the naked eye. His reflexes were aided by the adrenaline pumping through his body, allowing him to squeeze the trigger two times in quick succession without having to stop the motion of his hand.

When the Colt finally did come to a stop, one second had gone by. Smoke drifted up from the barrel as both shots were still ringing through the air, having come so quickly that they'd sounded like one.

Once again, silence started to descend upon the scene. This time, however, Ben was plainly shaken and confused.

"What's the matter with you?" he asked the men beside him.

As if to answer his question, both men slumped backward as blood soaked into the fronts of their shirts. Apparently, they'd been hit so fast that not even they fully realized what had happened. Their faces were expressionless and their bodies toppled over. Each had taken a single round through the heart.

Ben saw that his men were gone and turned to look back at Clint. The anger in his eyes was so intense that it seemed to burn through the air. He looked down the street and saw that, although he was beginning to stir, the man who'd been with the other half of the money didn't have a horse to ride on. In fact, the frightened animal was still running wildly on its way out of town.

The first set of saddlebags was on the back of the horse that was standing idly by. That one's rider was only now beginning to come around after falling completely into the water trough.

"In case you don't already know, it's over," Clint said.

Ben was so mad that he could barely move. "Yeah? Well then why don't you finish it?"

Clint pointed the Colt at the fat man, but didn't pull the trigger. "I don't have to finish it," he said. Nodding back toward the bank, he added, "They will."

At that moment, the sound of running footsteps closed in on the scene, followed by a rough, almost breathless voice. "Throw down yer guns," the voice said. "You're under arrest."

Before Ben could think about what to do next, he felt the cold touch of steel against the back of his skull, followed by strong hands roughly spinning him around. In the next instant, he was facing the reddened face of the sheriff as well as one of his deputies.

Although he couldn't see him, Ben could hear Clint's voice just fine.

"Can you take it from here?" Clint asked.

The lawman snatched the gun from Ben's hand as several more sets of footsteps came rushing closer. "The rest of my boys are here now, mister. We shouldn't have any trouble cleaning up this mess."

Clint holstered his Colt, but was ready to draw again at a moment's notice if any of the robbers looked like they still had any fight left in them. Although they looked angry enough to bite the heads off of each and every one of those lawmen, the bank robbers knew better than to make any wrong moves when Clint, the sheriff and two

deputies were all itching for a reason to put a bullet between their eyes.

The deputies gathered up the robbers and disarmed
them all. There were only three left that needed to be
handcuffed rather than buried. Once the smoke had settled, all of the fight seemed to have drained from the out-
laws' spirits.

Clint watched the sheriff's men work until the last of
the robbers were taken in. By then, the sheriff himself had
walked up to him and extended his hand.

"Name's Al Durrey. And after what I saw, I owe you
one hell of a thanks."

Clint took the lawman's hand and shook it. "Glad I
could be a help, Sheriff. I'm Clint Adams."

Now that the sheriff had gotten some of his breath back
after chasing the bank robbers, his words were coming a
lot easier than when he'd spoken to Ben. "Clint Adams,
is it? After that fine bit of shooting, I don't doubt that one
bit. Even so, I'll have to ask for that gun."

"Are you sure about that, Sheriff? There might still be
some of those men about."

The lawman seemed hesitant, but nodded. "I appreciate
the offer, but we've got everything under control."

Although Clint wasn't sure if Durrey had said that to
him or to the crowd that was closing in around the scene
of all the excitement, he handed over his Colt without a
fuss. "I'll be back for that."

Durrey studied the custom-made pistol with genuine
admiration. "I don't blame you. It'll be at my office waiting for you once we get this all straightened out. Standard
procedure. Especially when you gunned down a few of
these here criminals yourself rather than wait for us. I'm
sure you understand."

Clint may have understood, but that didn't mean he had
to like it. Still, he had other guns . . .

Watching the sheriff walk away and the deputies take

in the diminished gang, Clint waited until none of the lawmen were looking in his direction before stooping down as if to check the heel of his boot. Laying on the ground just behind the water trough was a small .32-caliber pistol which must have been dropped by the horseman he'd tackled.

I understand procedure, Sheriff, Clint thought as he took the weapon, slipped it under his shirt and stuck it behind his waistband. *I also understand how a killer thinks.*

The .32 was a battered holdout weapon at best, but it was better than nothing and almost as good as his own similar Colt New Line. Now he wouldn't have to go and dig that one out of his saddlebag. He knew better than to assume that the entire gang had been taken out, even though that seemed to be the case. If his experience had taught him anything, it was that any survivors of the fat man's group would be out for blood.

His blood, to be precise.

Procedure be damned, Clint wasn't going to let anyone come after his blood without a fight.

TEN

Clint watched the deputies go about their work while keeping an eye out for any stragglers that might have been left behind. If there were any members of the gang that had gotten away, however, they were smart enough to keep themselves hidden.

Before too long, Clint realized that it was more likely that any survivors of the gang would still be riding as fast as they could away from town. In fact, the more Clint's heart rate slowed to a more normal level, the more he realized that all the excitement was over for the day.

The notion that there were any more of the gang still at large was just something that nagged at the back of Clint's mind like a buzzing fly. It could have been caused by any number of things. After all, he'd felt that same peculiar nagging when he'd seen the fat man and his partner keep their posts across the street from his hotel.

Of course, the fact that those suspicions had panned out didn't ease Clint's mind in the least.

By this time, the last deputy had gone away and the undertaker had come for the bodies. Rather than stand around and second-guess that man's work as well, Clint headed back for his hotel. When he started walking, he felt his thoughts settle inside his mind and his blood slow to its normal pace.

No matter how much experience he'd had with trading lead, it was still not something he took lightly. There was still the nervousness and anxiousness he felt whenever he took that Colt from its holster. And though he knew how to get himself past the idea that his life was on the line, Clint was still affected by it.

He just needed to relax and unwind. That came as a funny thought considering how he'd spent the first part of his day.

Suddenly, Clint froze in his tracks and felt a wave of angry heat pulse through his system.

He knew what had been eating away at him just then. In fact, he was surprised he'd let the thought slip as far toward the back of his mind as it had. There definitely *was* another member of that gang walking around free as a bird.

That person might not have drawn a gun on him or taken a shot at any lawmen, but she was a part of the fat man's plan. In fact, she was the part specifically designed to keep Clint out of the way while the entire robbery went down.

Just thinking about what Natalia had done made him quicken his pace to get back to the hotel. By the time he got to the lobby, his blood was just about to boil.

He didn't notice any of the looks he got from the locals as he stormed through the door and headed for the stairs. Some of them might have tried to say something to him, but Clint was too focused to notice much of anything. The moment his feet hit the stairs, he flew up to the second floor and charged toward his door.

When he barged into the room he'd rented, Clint found exactly what he'd been expecting: absolutely nothing.

Actually, all of his possessions were still there, but that was not what he was looking for. Natalia—as well as any trace of her—had been completely wiped away from the room. The only thing to prove that she'd been there at all was the lingering scent of her expensive perfume which still hung in the air like a specter.

Clint walked over to the bed and sat down on its edge. It felt good to rest after the extended burst of energy that he'd put himself through, but that only lasted for a moment. Just touching that bed made him think about the woman he'd shared it with for the last couple of days.

All that time . . . she'd been playing him for a fool.

All that time . . . she'd probably been reporting back to that fat man whenever she wasn't keeping Clint busy.

All that time . . . Clint had been playing by someone else's rules.

It didn't matter that the robber's plan ultimately failed. What pissed Clint off more than anything was that he'd been suckered.

Sure, the plan hadn't been too complex or even too original, but Clint hadn't seen it coming until it was damn near too late.

He jumped up from the bed and immediately started gathering his things. Stuffing clothes and his few other belongings into his own saddlebag, Clint couldn't wait to get the hell out that room. The smell of the bitch stung his nostrils like acid. In fact, he couldn't wait to get out of that town.

There was a soft knocking coming from the door which caught Clint's ear. It wasn't much at first, but it got louder and faster when it repeated.

Clint wheeled around to look at who was making the noise and saw someone poking his head in from the hallway. It was a skinny, rat-faced man in his thirties who didn't look familiar at first. But when he saw that he'd been noticed and showed himself a bit more, the man struck a familiar chord in Clint's mind. He worked the front desk of the hotel and had been the one to check Clint in when he'd first arrived in town.

"Uhh . . . excuse me, Mr. Adams?" the clerk said uncertainly.

Clint stopped what he was doing and took a deep breath. "Yeah?"

"I just . . . wanted to—"

"Come on in here," Clint interrupted. "I'd rather not talk to just half a face and a door frame."

The clerk seemed a little embarrassed when he shuffled the rest of the way into Clint's room. "Mr. Adams, on behalf of some of the other folks in town . . . I'd like to thank you fer what you done."

Stopping in mid-tirade, Clint suddenly felt a little foolish for wanting to storm out of there in such a rush. He still felt angry for being played by Natalia, but now that he'd been pulled out of his own thoughts for a moment, he felt more like himself again.

"You saved a lot of lives back there," the clerk went on. "Some of us would like to treat you to a celebration. Maybe some drinks and a free meal."

The clerk seemed to be reacting to the anger which still lingered on Clint's face like a shadow. Once Clint took a moment to calm down a bit, some of that anger faded.

"I'd be honored," Clint said with a weary smile.

Acknowledging the smile with one of his own, the clerk brightened up immediately. He let out a short breath and even straightened his posture so that he didn't look like he was cowering anymore. In fact, the change was so drastic that the clerk seemed to have been replaced with another man entirely.

"Well, that's great," he said. "If there's anything you need or anything I can get for you . . . just let me know."

"Actually, there's two things."

"Name 'em."

"First of all, I'd appreciate a different room."

The clerk seemed a little puzzled by that one, but he shook it off quickly. By the look on his face, he was relieved to hear such an easy request. "Fine, fine. I've got a suite open that's perfect for a hero like you."

Even after all that had happened, Clint had to laugh when he heard that. "You can ease up on the royal treatment, uh . . ."

"Phil," the clerk said once he realized what Clint was waiting for. "My name's Phil."

"No need to tiptoe around me, Phil. But don't think that I'm letting you out of that free meal you promised me."

Phil grinned and nodded, feeling completely at ease by now. "You said there was something else I could do for you?"

"Yeah, Phil. You remember that woman that was staying with me? I'd like to know where she went."

ELEVEN

None of the three robbers said a word while they were being marched down to the sheriff's office. Only one of the men who'd been thrown from their horses made any noise at all, but that was just a few grunts of pain when he was forced to step too heavily on a twisted ankle.

Once the door to his jail cell slammed shut, Ben glared at the sheriff from between the bars and said, "When's my trial?"

Sheriff Durrey returned the fat man's stare and stepped up so that his nose almost brushed against the iron bars. His eyes burned with a rage that he just barely managed to contain, and when he spoke, his words seeped out of him like steam from a furnace.

"Those bank guards were friends of mine," the lawman said. "They're both dead and for all I know you're the one who pulled the trigger on each of them."

Ben shrugged and flashed the sheriff one of his beaming, gap-toothed smiles. "I fired at so many of you law dog sons-of-bitches that I barely remember. Hell, I might've been the one to put them two out of their misery. Guess I don't really give a shit if it was or not."

Both of the sheriff's arms shot between the bars so he

could take hold of the front of Ben's shirt. With strength that came from Durrey's rage just as much as his muscles, he pulled the bank robber forward until Ben's face slammed against the bars.

"Look here, you piece of horseshit," the sheriff growled. "If you're trying to get yourself shot before you even see the inside of a courthouse, then you just keep talking."

"I ain't gonna see no judge."

"Maybe you're not as dumb as you look, asshole. Because even if I restrain myself enough to keep from killing you, I doubt I'll have enough left to hold back the lynch mob that'll be coming for your sorry hide sooner or later."

There wasn't the first hint of fear in Ben's eyes. Instead, he looked back at the sheriff with mild uninterest. That smile was still hanging on his face, which he could tell was stoking the lawman's fires even more.

"You got anything else to say to me?" Ben asked.

"Yeah. How much longer are you going to be able to smile with a broken nose?"

With that, Sheriff Durrey pushed the bank robber back a few inches and then pulled him forward with all the strength his arms could manage. Ben tried to turn his head, but he wasn't quick enough to do so before his face slammed into the unyielding metal bars. The wet crunch of breaking cartilage sounded throughout the confines of the cell, taking the smile away from Ben's face and putting it squarely onto the sheriff's.

"Y'all sit tight now," Durrey said with satisfaction as he let go of Ben's shirt. "I'll send your dinners as soon as I get around to it."

The sheriff turned away from the prisoners and walked out of the jail. Since the building wasn't even as big as a normal house, it only took him three or four steps before he was outside. The walls may have been close together, but they were thick and well maintained. As soon as Durrey shut and latched the door, nearly all the sound from the outside world was immediately cut off.

Ben had been gripping the bars with both hands and staring at the sheriff's back so intently that he was expecting to see smoke curl up from the lawman's jacket. When the outer door closed, Ben's knuckles turned white and his teeth clenched together so hard that it quickened the flow of blood from his smashed nose.

For a few seconds, the jailhouse was as quiet as a crypt.

Soon, the raspy sound of forced breathing could be heard, followed by a churning rumble originating from the bottom of Ben's throat. As that rumble got louder, it took on more of an animalistic quality, building into a savage, furious roar.

Shouting until his lungs were empty, Ben peeled his hands off the bars and balled them into large, chunky fists. That done, he turned away from the cell door and stomped toward the back wall. One of the two other men from his gang to make it through the gunfight was in the same cell, slumped onto the rickety cot.

"Jesus, Ben are you all—"

The robber's question was cut off by a swift backhand from his partner. Ben's knuckles smacked across the other man's mouth and nearly knocked his jaw out of place.

"Don't you even ask if I'm all right," Ben snarled. "Because that would be the dumbest thing you could possibly say right now."

Since he'd already been unsteady on his feet after having been knocked from his horse, the other man fell against the wall and lost consciousness for a few seconds. When he shook some sense back into his head, he rubbed the side of his face with the back of his hand. His temper flared, but he didn't have the strength to back it up.

Ben's eyes never left the other man's face until he was certain he'd successfully shut him up. Nodding slowly when there was no challenge forthcoming, he stalked to the other side of the cell to get a look at the cage next to his own.

Sitting in that one, quietly watching what was going on, was the man who'd been tackled and dropped into the water trough. Although he didn't say anything to the fat man, his eyes were narrow, angry slits.

"What's on your mind?" Ben asked. "You got something to say or are you just gonna sit there trying to scare me with that bad look of yours?"

"Screaming ain't going to help nothing," the man in the other cell said. "Thanks to you, we're all dead no matter what."

Ben cocked his head to one side and pressed himself against the bars as though he was about to reach across and strangle his fellow prisoner. "Thanks to me, huh? Was that me who nearly broke his damn neck falling into horse water? Funny . . . I don't think it was."

The other man didn't argue any further. Instead, he shook his head, turned on his cot so that he had his back to the fat man and closed his eyes.

"Don't you turn your back on me, you son of a bitch!" Ben hollered.

Exasperated, Ben slammed his fist against the bars. He then turned toward the wall and slammed his fist against the bricks. No matter how much anger he brewed up, he couldn't get away from the fact that what his men had said was absolutely right.

They were going to die.

No matter what.

TWELVE

"A tale told by idiots."

The woman in the back of the room fussed with her hair while staring at her reflection in a grimy mirror. "What?" she asked while shifting her eyes to look at another reflection besides her own.

Sitting at the small vanity, she picked up a comb that was missing a few of its teeth and ran it through her hair. Her chair was wobbly, yet served its function well enough, just like most of the other girls who worked the saloon on the first floor of this same building.

The rest of the room was cluttered with battered furniture, most of its space taken up by a large, four-poster bed. Since the room's very existence was to enclose that bed, it was no wonder that it was the finest piece of furnishing in there. Even so, the woman spent more time at her vanity, gazing once again at her reflection once she saw that she wasn't about to get an answer to her question anytime soon.

The man stood at the window, holding open the yellowed curtains with a casual index finger. His head slumped forward on his shoulders, giving him the appearance of an inanimate figure that had been propped up and leaned against the wall. Even the words he'd spoken sounded thin and hollow, like something that had been said days ago and was only now echoing through the room.

That forward-slouching head shook back and forth. If there had been any wind in the room, the woman might have thought that was what caused the motion. But there was nothing more than a slight trickle of air seeping in through the tiny crack between the bottom of the window and its sill, just enough to clean out the stale smell of sex which permanently hung within those four particular walls.

"I said it's a tale told by idiots," the man repeated. "Full of sound and fury . . . signifying nothing."

Still fussing with her hair, the woman nodded. "Oh. That's kind of pretty. Did you make that up?"

If she'd bothered to look at him, the woman could not have missed the look of blatant disgust on the man's face when he turned to glance in her direction. He studied her through narrowed eyes with as much regard as he might have for a pig that lifted its nose up from a pile of slop.

"Yeah," he said, deciding that she wasn't worth any further explanation. "I made it up."

The literary quote already forgotten, she gave him an approving smile and went back to her hair.

No matter how much he truly despised ignorance, the man had to laugh quietly at the woman's unapologetic stupidity. She didn't know what the hell he was talking about and didn't care who knew it. He might have hated ignorance, but perhaps it truly was bliss.

He turned his attention back to the window and peered outside. By the looks of things, the commotion from the gunfight at the bank was starting to die down. The bullets had stopped flying some time ago and the robbers had all been carted away either by the sheriff or the undertaker.

That didn't leave much else for the locals to do besides

stand around and gab about what they'd seen and heard. He couldn't make out more than the occasional word from directly beneath his window, but the man knew that most of them were excitedly chattering about the one who was most responsible for stopping the robbery.

When he thought about that one, the man idly ran the tip of his tongue along the sharp edges of his teeth. Just like Ben Scott, he knew that Clint Adams was in town. After all, any gunman who wanted to stay alive did so by keeping track of his competition.

Clint Adams was more than just competition. He was a legitimate threat. And the only way to overcome a legitimate threat was to either beat it down or get out of its way.

Ben must have thought he'd come up with a third option by trying to make sure that Adams got out of *his* way. The man at the window didn't think for a moment that such a plan had any chance of working, but he'd been curious enough to watch and see all the same. Unfortunately, he hadn't seen anything outside of what he'd been expecting. Although that was a comforting stroke to his ego, it didn't make for very interesting entertainment.

And just when he thought about entertainment, the man heard his own little diversion getting up from her vanity and making her way to stand behind him. Her hands ran along his back and slipped around his waist. He could feel her plump breasts pushing against him as her fingers slid up and down his chest.

"How much longer are you going to stand at that window?" she asked.

"Why, darling? Are you getting bored?"

The man didn't have any illusions that she truly liked being called by such an affectionate name, but he did so anyway because he hadn't bothered trying to remember her real one.

She played up to it all the same, giggling in a way that

endeared her to most of her customers while also loosening their purse strings in the process. "I'm never bored with a big man like you. Actually, I was hoping you'd want to keep me around for a bit longer." Her hand slipped between his legs, massaging the bulge in his crotch until she felt it harden beneath her fingers. "I can make it worth your while," she purred.

"I'm sure you can."

"So how about it?" she asked, her hands moving up to his elbows so she could pull him away from the window. "I want you to make me scream like you did last time."

The man didn't pull away from her, but he also didn't budge from his spot. Even as she pulled him a little harder, he stayed right where he was as though he'd been rooted in that spot. "When I want some more of you," he said while shrugging out of her insistent grasp, "I'll come find you."

He reached into his pocket and pulled out a silver dollar. "Here," he said after flipping the dollar over his shoulder. "Take this and go away."

She let go of him as though he'd suddenly been covered with fire ants. Propping her hands on her hips, she was about to spit a profanity in his direction when she looked down at the coin which spun near her right foot. She kept the name she was about to call him inside and picked up her money.

The man standing at the window listened to her walk away, open the door, step outside, and then shut the door behind her. Part of him was mildly disappointed that she hadn't had the guts to say what she really thought of him. Depending on what venom had come out of her mouth, he might have either taken her up on her offer or beaten her senseless.

But she was gone now, so rather than waste his time thinking about her, he turned his attention back to the reason he was in Willett in the first place.

That reason had just come out of the hotel across the street, led by the hotel's owner and greeted by the locals as their new hero.

Clint Adams didn't play up to the small crowd that had gathered down there. He never did. In fact, he seemed more than a little uncomfortable with all the attention. On the other hand, he didn't seem to mind it very much either.

The man watched Adams go outside and graciously accept the handshakes and pats on the back that came at him from all sides. Rather than encourage any more of the worshipping behavior, Adams led the way into the saloon downstairs and disappeared from the man's view.

"What a fucking hero," the man growled.

THIRTEEN

On the way over to the saloon across the street, Clint realized that Phil was the hotel's owner on top of being the man who sat behind the desk for most of the day. He told Clint that he thought Natalia might be in the saloon and then proceeded to take him there personally.

Once he stepped outside and into the midst of a crowd that had gathered in the space of a few minutes, Clint began to think that he'd been told about the saloon just so that he would agree to go over there. Indeed, Phil wasn't concerned with much of anything except moving Clint along and trading excited words with some of the more boisterous locals.

Clint felt uncomfortable almost immediately. It was nice to have so many folks wanting to shake his hand and congratulate him on a job well done, but it all seemed a bit too much for his tastes.

"Hey, Phil," Clint said once he'd made it to the saloon's front door. "Is that woman I asked you about really in here?"

The hotel owner stopped short and a guilty expression crossed onto his face. Shifting his eyes back and forth, he pushed Clint onward until they were both inside. "If she

52

isn't . . . I'll bet someone in here knows where to look. But don't worry about her, Mr. Adams. I'm sure she'll want to find you before too long at all." Leaning in a little closer, he winked and added, "There's plenty of gals who'd like to meet you, I'm sure."

Clint tried not to look agitated with the other man. "I really want to find her," he said. "It's actually rather important—"

The rest of what Clint was trying to say was washed out in a flood of sound. Everything from slamming doors to thumping footsteps filled the saloon, all of which was blended with a constant flow of chattering voices. The locals all swarmed into the place and got as close to Clint as they could manage. Every one of them had a question they wanted to ask, ranging from the bank robbery to famous people Clint might know.

Knowing that the people meant well, Clint fielded the questions as best he could as the first of many free drinks was set in front of him. Looking at the zoo that had formed around him, Clint realized that if Natalia didn't want to be found, she'd be long gone by now. And if she did want to be found, she would have no problem knowing where to be.

So Clint shook his head and lifted his glass in response to a toast spoken in his honor. After the day he'd had, he didn't have the inclination to refuse a few free beers. And once he'd played up to the crowd just a little bit, most of the locals drifted off to engage in their own conversations. Only Phil stayed next to Clint the whole time and didn't move from the bar once the excitement settled down a bit.

Clint had finished his first beer and handed the empty glass over to the balding bartender. After topping off the glass, the barkeep nodded to Clint and moved off to tend to the rest of the customers that had descended upon the place.

Standing at the bar, Phil sipped at a shot of whiskey.

His wide eyes moved around the place as though he was in awe at the number of people packed into the saloon. When he looked back over to Clint, he lifted his whiskey and tossed it off, trying desperately not to hack it back up.

Clint suppressed a grin at the hotel owner's attempted display of manliness and instead took a healthy swallow of his own drink to return the gesture. "So tell me, Phil," he said once both of their glasses were back on top of the bar. "Does this town see a lot of excitement?"

"Not really. There was some trouble with some bandits raiding coaches and such on the road from New York City, but Sheriff Durrey rousted them out. That was . . . upward of two years ago now.

"Other than that, it's not much more than the usual kind of thing. Saloon brawls, some drunkenness and a shooting every now and then, but nothing like today. No sir, nothing like today."

Clint could sense another round of excited reminiscing about to spring from the hotel owner, so he quickly steered clear. "Now about that woman I wanted to find . . ."

"Oh yes. Her name was . . . Natalia, wasn't it?"

"Yes, it was. Is she from around here?"

Phil thought about that for a second before shrugging his shoulders. "I don't think so, but that shouldn't get you too discouraged. I see so many faces day in and day out that they all seem to blend together after a while. She might be new in town." Once again, that guilty look came onto his face. "Or . . . she might be passing through."

This time, Clint didn't try to hide the annoyance he was feeling. "So you were lying before about knowing where she went?"

"Not lying so much. Most folks that stay at my hotel come here for drinks or a meal. Besides . . . I . . . I knew that some folks wanted to express their gratitude for what you did." Slapping the top of the bar with his hand, Phil quickly added, "And now that you're here, I'll see what I can do to find that lady. I'm a man of my word, Mr. Adams. The least I can do is help you out after what you did today. My life savings is in that bank, right along with plenty of others'. Yes sir, it'd be my honor to help you."

Clint had been studying the other man's face as he was talking. After what had happened with Natalia, he wasn't about to let anyone else pull anything over on him. The only reason she'd been able to get anything past him was that Clint hadn't been as alert as he should have been.

In the scheme of things, Natalia hadn't really done too much. But Clint knew better than anybody that even the simplest of mistakes could prove to be disastrous. Turning your back at the wrong time was a good way to get a bullet in it, which was why Clint wasn't so quick to just forget about Natalia altogether.

But even as wary as he was feeling about the motives of others at the moment, Clint would have been hard pressed to think that Phil was trying to do anything but what he said he was going to do. And perhaps it was the beers, but Clint was also starting to ease off on the urgent need to find Natalia and confront her with what she'd done.

"All right," Clint said to the hotel owner. "I'd appreciate your help, but you don't have to go running off just yet."

"Are you sure? Because it's the least I could do, especially after—"

"I know," Clint interrupted in a way he hoped wasn't too rude. "Just keep your eye out for her and let me know if she comes around. There's no need to knock yourself out over it, since she probably won't be coming back here anytime soon anyway."

Phil looked a bit confused. "Not coming back? Why?"

"Let's just say she got the job done that she was getting

paid for, so she probably doesn't have a whole lot of reasons to stick around."

After hearing that, Phil got a wry grin on his face and started nodding slowly. "Ahhhh," he said knowingly. "Now I see what you're talking about. Is that lady one of the ones that . . . uhhh . . . works in here?"

Clint laughed and shook his head. "No. At least . . . I don't think so. That's not the kind of job I meant."

"Oh." Although he was doing his best not to look that way, it was obvious that Phil was once again confused. "Well . . . if I hear about her or see her around, you'll be the first to know, Mr. Adams."

Glad to hear the last of that subject for a while, Clint raised his glass. "I'll drink to that."

Before he knew it, the entire bar came alive with dozens of voices shouting their agreement to whatever Clint had decided to toast. The locals cheered and raised their own glasses, even though they couldn't have had the slightest notion what Clint had been saying.

Shaking his head, Clint decided to enjoy his status for a little while longer and be the first to take a drink of his uplifted beer. The whole bar drank with him and then went back to their conversations.

"Now this," Clint said to the smiling hotel owner, "has been one hell of a day."

FOURTEEN

With spring fresh in the air and summer not too far behind, the days were getting longer and the air was getting warmer. More folks were taking their time walking along the streets when the sun melted into the horizon after an inspired blood-red and deep-purple display.

Willett wasn't a town of much import, but it was a stop along the trail to New York City. Therefore, it got more than its fair share of trading caravans and travelers. The stagecoaches rattled along the town's streets well into that night, and whenever a new arrival stepped down from a carriage or swung out of a saddle, the newcomer was given at least a quick telling of what had transpired earlier that day.

By the end of the day the story had been told a hundred or so times. The gunfight had become even more spectacular, while most of the actual details had been rubbed away like the polish on a frequently turned doorknob. Clint's name was mentioned less and less. After a while, whoever told the story inserted the name of whatever famous gunman he or she liked best, swearing that it was the God's honest truth. Not that the locals were lying out of spite or any bad intentions. They'd simply caught themselves up in their own story and wanted to believe anything at all to make that story more exciting.

As he walked down the street, Mark Rackton drifted from person to person, allowing them to tell him their own versions of what had happened. As he listened to the newest version of the truth, Mark plastered an interested look onto his face and nodded just to keep them talking. No matter what babble they spewed, it was a hell of a lot better than standing in his room above the saloon watching that damn whore comb her hair.

Rackton stood just over six feet tall and had a muscular build hiding beneath his loose-fitting clothes. Wiry muscles clung to his bones, but he did a good job of carrying himself in a distinctly ordinary way. The best way for him to be stronger, he'd decided a long time ago, was to keep whatever strength he had to himself. That way, he wasn't so easy to size up. And that, he knew, was one of the best strengths a man could have.

His clothes were simple, yet refined. Plain black pants and a starched white shirt beneath a pearl-gray vest. Above that was a knee-length waistcoat, and he topped it all with a black Stetson to cover a scalp he shaved himself every couple days or so.

All in all, he looked better than some cowboy fresh off the trail, but not rich enough to draw any undue attention. His eyes were a cold, steely blue, always absorbing every last detail around him. His lean face was covered with a thick goatee, hiding the sunken features almost as well as his clothes hid his muscular build.

Once he'd heard all one local had to say about the day's events, Rackton moved on. He hadn't started out walking in any particular direction when he'd first stepped into the cool, fragrant air. All he'd wanted was to stretch his legs for a while before making his way to his real destination.

He was constantly amazed by just how far the same story got stretched. After a while, he started to wonder if he'd ever created a stir anywhere close to this in the towns where he'd left his mark. Rackton doubted that very much, since most of the people who knew his true nature were either working with him or dead.

More often than not, they'd started out as one and wound up the other.

Idly tapping the ground next to his left foot with a walking stick he'd picked up in New York City, Rackton sidled away from the man unloading a newly arrived stagecoach. He knew he wouldn't be missed since he'd left behind all the coach's passengers to listen to the man's tale. Once he was clear of the group, Rackton reached into his vest pocket and removed a silver watch attached to a chain.

It was nearly eight o'clock. Soon, he would have to cut his nightly walk short and get back down to the business at hand.

When he dropped the pocket watch back into its place, he pulled open his coat just enough to reveal a .44 revolver with a handle plated in ivory hanging in a rig beneath his left arm. The weapon's identical twin hung beneath Rackton's right arm, but could hardly be seen at all thanks to the cut of his jacket which had been specifically tailored to conceal the double shoulder rig.

Filling his lungs with a deep, soothing breath, he rounded the corner and started making his way back to the saloon which had been the center for much of the commotion following the bank robbery. Rackton's room was above that place, but he wouldn't be heading back there right away.

Instead, he was more interested in checking in at the saloon itself. He was there in a matter of minutes and was surprised to see that many of the same faces that had been there before were still there now. Usually, Rackton found that the average person's attention span was about the same as a yapping dog's. If it didn't have to do with one of their basic needs, folks tended to forget about it the moment it was out of their sight. Sometimes, even before.

But such was not the case this time. In fact, the impromptu gathering had turned into a small event. Rackton was pleased when he spotted one familiar face in particular. Apparently, Clint Adams wasn't half as shy as he'd been acting earlier in the day. He was talking it up with a group of men at a card table. Although they seemed to be playing something, they seemed more interested in their animated discussion.

Rackton couldn't care less what they were talking about, just so long as they kept at it for a while longer. He was just about to turn away from the entrance to the saloon when he felt something knock into his side.

The impact wasn't enough to do any harm, but it was enough to cause Rackton to extend his arm and the walking stick he was holding.

" 'Scuse me, mister," the man who'd bumped into Rackton said. "You mind stepping out of the way?"

Rackton locked eyes with the other man and started to move aside. At the last moment, he snapped his arm back out while flicking his wrist sharply upward. The motion caused his walking stick to fly up through his grasp until he stopped it with a quick clench of his fist.

Holding the stick's polished steel head just beneath the other man's chin, Rackton moved completely in front of him so that nobody could get through the door. In a low, hissing voice, he said, "You should watch where you're going. Or do you just expect the rest of the goddamn world to step aside for you?"

When Rackton had first stepped in his way, the other man looked as though he was about to lose his temper. His face twisted into an angry scowl and his hands balled up into fists. But when he looked into Rackton's face, his anger started to look more like a weak facade. His chin trembled ever so slightly before he spoke. "Easy, stranger. Just trying to get by."

Rackton intensified his stare until the other man blinked and looked away. He then snapped the walking stick up just enough to rap the other man's chin before moving to one side. Watching as the man hurried into the saloon, Rackton turned his back on the door and resumed his walk. It didn't take long for his steps to regain their easy gait, and soon he was even whistling softly to himself as he made his way down the street.

In one part of his mind, he could still feel that loser's shoulder bumping against him as though he wasn't even there. It would have felt so good to do that bastard a little more damage, but then Rackton figured he might not have gotten everything done that he'd wanted to do that evening.

In the other part of his mind, Rackton was planning out what he still had to do. There was a big job ahead of him, and at the end of it, he would square things up with another son of a bitch whom he owed a thing or two.

"You just keep playing your cards and drinking your drinks," he said to himself. "After all . . . every dying man deserves his final day in the sun. Even you, Clint Adams."

FIFTEEN

After Clint had been at the saloon for a while longer, Sheriff Durrey wandered through the front door and walked straight up to him. The lawman seemed fairly subdued, but also a little uncomfortable the further he walked into the place.

"I've got something of yours, Adams," the lawman said. He handed over the modified Colt. "Considering the circumstances, I guess I don't have much reason to keep hold of it. It's not like that was just some bar fight or something."

Clint holstered the Colt and said, "Thanks, Sheriff. Can I buy you a drink?"

"Nah. I'm not one for crowds. 'Sides, I've got my rounds to make. Keep out of trouble." With that, the sheriff tipped his hat and left the saloon.

There were plenty of locals willing to fill the empty spot next to Clint, but none of them wanted to talk about anything except for the bank robbery. With a little coaxing, Clint managed to turn the tide of the conversation away from himself and onto some topics that were more to his liking. It wasn't long at all before poker came up. Once that happened, it was just a few minutes more until the gathering was moved to one of the card tables in the saloon and the first hand was dealt.

The stakes were nothing special. In fact, they were some of the lowest that Clint had played for in a long time. But the pot wasn't his main reason for staying in the game. The locals were actually nice people who gave him a run for what little money wound up on the middle of the table. The conversation was entertaining and the free beers kept on flowing.

Yes indeed, Clint was definitely starting to warm up to Willett, New York.

It took less than another hour of playing before the locals at the table got up the confidence to start raising the stakes. The first one to start down that road was a man in his early twenties with light brown hair and a face smoother than the side of a satin pillow. He'd been one of the quieter players until it came for him to bet.

They were playing seven card draw, and the young man, Billy, sat on Clint's left and had two sevens showing.

"And the baby face takes the lead," Clint said, using the nickname he'd given to the younger man.

Although the jibes were good natured, they seemed to get under Billy's skin just enough to make calling him that name worthwhile. Billy had a decent poker face, but cracked a little whenever someone called him that.

His lips tightening with mild annoyance, Billy threw in enough to cover the bet. After pausing for effect, he said, "And make it three dollars more."

At times, the entire pot of the game had added up to less than a dollar. After Billy had pushed in his money, the entire table groaned with exaggerated despair.

Emmett, a skinny shopkeeper with a face full of scraggly, salt-and-pepper whiskers, whistled softly and shook his head. "Lordy, lordy. It looks like the kid wants to grow up and be a man. What's next, Billy? Think you're ready to rub that smooth face of yours against a real girl?"

The rest of the table laughed at Emmett's natural ability to get under Billy's skin. It wasn't that his jokes were that funny, but the effect they had on the kid was amusing in itself. Amusing to everyone except Billy, of course.

"Just shut yer mouth and play, Emmett," Billy replied. "Or are you too scared to hang in there with a baby face like me?"

That alone earned Billy a bit of the respect he felt he'd been losing the entire night. Clint nodded and smirked with approval, looking over to Emmett for the other man's response.

"All right, little man, no need to get cross," Emmett said. "I guess I can let you have this one." And with that, he folded the two cards he'd been holding and tossed them onto his deuce and nine of clubs.

That pleased Billy to no end, and he puffed his chest out as though he'd won the entire game. "How about you, Sam?" he said, shifting his eyes to the next man in line to bet. "You got the sand to hang in there when the stakes go up?"

Sam had the look of a lifelong range rider who'd only recently been tamed enough for life in town. His long, silvery hair had the texture of wire and the color of dull gunmetal. It hung down past his shoulders in something slightly better than a complete tangle, matching the thick, bushy mustache sprawling over his upper lip.

His eyes were sharp and full of fire, yet he spoke in a distinctly subdued tone. "Oh, I think I can manage to call," he said, the thick mustache hiding any movement of his lips. He tossed in a stack of chips while his eyes remained locked on the kid. "Looks like I misjudged my numbers there, Baby Face. I'd say there's two buck more in there than I needed. Might as well let 'em stay there. It should keep Clint honest at least."

Clint looked at the other man and nodded slowly. A

grin crept onto his lips as he cocked his head to one side. Sam was showing the five and six of hearts compared to his own pair of fours. "Five dollars, huh? Well, I hate to break this to you, Sam, but I don't stay honest for anything less than eight." Clint slid the stack of chips out onto the table, watching Sam's face for any sign that might give him some insight into what the older man was holding.

But Sam's face was nothing more than a hardened mask of deeply etched lines and leathery skin. He didn't flinch at the raise. The only thing he did do was return Clint's smile while staring right back at him.

Clint knew he was being studied as well. After all, that was part of the art of poker. Beyond the lay of the cards and the luck of the draw, the ultimate test was a man's grasp on human nature. Looking into another player's eyes and seeing if you could tell what was going on in there was the real skill behind poker. The rest of it could be delegated to Lady Luck.

Another skill involved the not-so-fine art of cheating at cards. Clint might not have done that himself, but he knew enough to spot it when it was being done to him. For the moment, the current game was still a friendly one and the first skill was the only one truly concerning Clint.

Sam had obviously had plenty of practice in that skill as well, because Clint couldn't read much more than the smile on the other man's face. He could appreciate a challenge and decided to wait and see the old-fashioned way what Sam was holding.

The youngest player wasn't half as hard to read. "Shit," Billy muttered. "I guess I'll stay in."

Since Billy didn't seem to have much trouble pushing the last of his chips into the center of the table, Clint figured that Baby Face had to have something else in his hold cards that was giving him enough confidence to go on.

With nothing more than a slight shrug, Sam tossed in enough to cover the bet. "I'm in."

And then the next round of cards was dealt. Clint got a queen of diamonds. Billy got a jack and Sam tossed a seven of hearts down to match the five and six he already had showing. The older man's face barely shifted as he looked up at Billy from beneath shaggy eyebrows. "What you got to say for yerself now, Baby Face?"

Billy glanced at Clint and Sam's cards, trying not to look nervous. His expression slipped for a moment, which was just long enough to tell Clint all he needed to know.

"Five," Billy said as he slid forward five dollars' worth of chips.

"Make it ten," Sam said without batting an eye.

Clint looked up at Sam as he said, "And ten again."

By now, the players had already gone past their supply of chips and were throwing bills and coins in to cover their bets. Clint didn't even have to look at Billy to know what the younger man was about to do.

Letting out a frustrated groan, Billy slapped his cards down onto the table.

SIXTEEN

Clint was truly enjoying himself. The air in the saloon was filled with the stale smell of alcohol and smoke. The sound of dozens of conversations mingled with the chatter of a piano that was half a note off-key. And thanks to the efforts of a redheaded waitress with a plump backside, the mug at his right hand was never empty.

All things considered, Clint felt like he'd found a little slice of heaven. "That just leaves you and me," he said to Sam.

The older man nodded once, his face still a nearly unreadable mask. "Sure does. And I'm the one that's got to keep you honest." Without saying anything else, he reached into his shirt pocket and pulled out enough bills to keep the game moving.

Once the next cards had been dealt, neither man had much of an improvement on his standing. Clint got an ace of clubs while Sam flipped himself the three of spades.

Only one card left to go, but it was that one that would affect the entire game.

It was dealt to each man face down. Clint looked at his only briefly and then set it down on top of his other two. In a way, he thought that his cards didn't matter. What really counted was whether or not he could figure out what was in the other players' hands. Beyond that, he just needed to make them *think* he had a good hand of his own.

Maybe he would have the cards.

Maybe he wouldn't.

Poker was all about finesse. Judging by the stony smile on Sam's face, he knew that every bit as much as Clint did. "It ain't much, but you got the best hand showing," Sam said.

"No," Clint replied honestly. "It isn't much. But, maybe I'm just crazy for liking it all the same." More as a way to prolong the moment, Clint took another peek at his three hold cards. Normally, he wouldn't have been excited about them at all. There wasn't so much as a pair in there, but he did have another four.

More importantly, it was the four of hearts. To make things even more interesting, he had the eight of hearts as well. With those cards in his hand, Clint knew for a fact that Sam couldn't possibly have his straight flush. And since he had three of the fours in the deck, odds were that Sam couldn't even have a straight unless he completely lucked out and got an eight and nine of some other suit.

Glancing around the table, Clint counted up from memory a couple of the nines laying scattered among Billy's and Emmett's discarded hands. Now the odds were even more in his favor, but Clint's face hadn't changed at all. In fact, he managed to look convincingly hesitant when he raised the bet.

"Since I'm in this far," Clint said, "I might as well hit you up for another ten."

For the first time since the game had started, Sam's face actually twitched. "All right, Clint. If you want to take advantage of an old man and his life savings, I won't stand in your way."

"Don't give me any of that, old man," Clint laughed. "Are you in or out?"

"In." Sam matched the bet and said, "What've you got?"

Clint shrugged and put down his cards. "Not a lot. But I do have three fours . . . along with the two cards you needed to fill out that straight flush of yours."

Sam shook his head. "I'll be damned. I shouldn't have tried to bluff you, eh? All I'm holding is a pair . . . of sevens." He set the pair next to his other seven and leveled his eyes at Clint. "What do you know about that?"

The entire table seemed to lose its breath for a moment. Clint sat back in his chair and took one last look at the impressive pile of money that had been built up in front of him. His face was still expressionless as he moved his hands in closer to himself and then lowered his eyes.

When Clint extended his hand, Billy actually twitched in his chair. He seemed surprised that Clint wasn't holding his Colt as he leaned toward Sam.

"Helluva game, old man," Clint said as he dropped the poker face and shook Sam's hand. "It was worth losing that cash just to see another pro at work."

The tensions at the table eased up as both men shook hands. Sam was the only one who hadn't seemed nervous in the least. As he shook Clint's hand, he grinned widely, causing the ends of his bushy mustache to curl upward like a squirming caterpillar. "That was the most exciting three of a kind I ever had. Next round's on me."

"You're damn right it is," Clint said. "And you're not going anywhere until I win some of that money back."

"You can *try* to win it back."

Clint gathered up the cards and started shuffling. He glared at Sam out of the corner of his eye and shook his head. "And after all I did for this town. You should be ashamed of yourself."

"Hey, my money wasn't in that bank," Sam shot back.

"Damn place isn't safe enough for my tastes."

The entire table laughed at that one. Clint chose five card draw for his game and dealt out the cards accordingly. Just as he was tossing down the last card, he saw someone approaching from the corner of his eye. He looked up just as the figure pulled out the chair right next to him and sat down.

"Is it too late for me to join you?" the well-proportioned blond woman said. "Or is this game for men only?"

"I don't know about the rest of these fellas," Clint said. "But I can't think of a single thing I'd turn you away from."

Her smile reflected the carefree attitude that made her eyes sparkle in a subtle, mischievous way. "My name's Anne Kielly."

"Clint Adams."

"I don't know about this Clint," Sam said in his baritone grumble. "This one's never been nothing but trouble."

Anne looked offended as she glanced over to the man sitting on her other side. Without missing a beat, she backhanded him on the shoulder. Sam smiled beneath his mustache and rubbed his arm like he'd just taken a bullet.

"See what I mean?" he said.

Clint studied her for a few moments before saying, "What the hell. I could always use a little more trouble in my life."

SEVENTEEN

Despite having more excitement in one day than he'd ever had in his entire career as a sheriff's deputy, Will Tannen was already starting to feel bored. Granted, he'd only been a deputy for a little over a year, but after getting a taste of some of what he'd signed on for in the first place, he was beginning to miss the frantic pace that had taken up the earlier part of his day.

Now that the bank was sealed up tight again and the surviving robbers were behind bars, all that remained was to keep an eye on them until the judge decided to convene a trial. Sitting with his feet propped up on Sheriff Durrey's desk, Will thought back to the gunfight.

Just the fact that he'd been in a gunfight at all was enough to make him feel like a big man. Until today, he'd never even had much of a reason to fire his pistol. It wasn't his first fight at all, but this was something special.

Men had been shooting at him.

He'd shot back at them.

He'd even chased them down a ways.

Even Clint Adams had been there, trading lead right with him. When Will thought about that, he actually started to swell with pride. Clint Adams. The Gunsmith. Hot damn.

"Do you know where I can find the sheriff?"

Hearing the question all of a sudden, Will's entire body flinched and he nearly spilled himself right out of his chair. Trying to cover the fact that he'd been taken so completely by surprise, the deputy grabbed hold of the chair and looked down at the legs in frustration.

"Damn chair," he muttered. "Been meaning to fix the thing, but I never got around to it." Satisfied that he'd covered his tracks as best he could, Will got to his feet and looked at the man who was standing just inside the office door. "What can I do for you?"

Mark Rackton watched the younger man fluster about like some kid who'd been caught with his hand in his pants. Not letting his amusement show, he said, "I'd like to see the sheriff. Is he here?"

Will looked the other man up and down. After summing him up using his professional lawman's eyes, he stepped around the desk and ushered him in. After all, the man looked like some kind of dandy. He even carried a cane like one of those fancy city types that came through town every so often.

"Sheriff Durrey is making his rounds," Will said. "He won't be back here until the morning. I can help you, though."

The deputy wasn't the only one sizing up the man in front of him. Rackton was also doing some studying of his own. The first thing he could tell was that the youthful lawman had just come to his own conclusions. Fortunately for Rackton, they appeared to be the wrong conclusions.

Judging by the way Will's features softened and he took a superior stance, Rackton knew that the deputy assumed he was in no danger and that he could handle whatever might come his way. Rackton played up to that and took the edge from his voice while placing both hands atop his cane.

"Were you involved with the incident at the bank?" Rackton asked, even though he already knew the answer.

Will didn't seem to mind the change in subject one bit. In fact, he latched onto it with both arms. "I certainly was. Right in the thick of it, you might say."

"Really? How terribly interesting. It's a shame what happened to those two guards."

Suddenly, the triumphant look on Will's face dimmed a bit and some of the bluster faded from his voice. "Yeah . . . it sure was. We got the sons of bitches that did it, though. The ones that ain't dead are locked up in the jailhouse. They'll get what's coming to them."

"I'm sure, I'm sure. Might I have a word with them?"

That snapped Will out of his revery. "You want to talk to the prisoners?"

"Is that a problem?" Rackton asked innocently.

"Who are you?"

The moment he'd gotten a good look at the deputy, Rackton had his approach planned out completely. Extending his hand, he smiled disarmingly and spoke with just the right amount of eagerness in his voice. "Kyle Worthington. I work for a newspaper that covers events in the New York area. You must have heard of the *New York Examiner*."

"The *Examiner*? Sure, I've heard of it," the deputy replied even though he'd never read any paper besides the one published two blocks away by a retired librarian.

"Ah, a man who knows his facts. But then again, any lawman who wants to stay alive under fire has got to keep himself sharp, hasn't he?"

"He does."

"I'm only in town until tomorrow. After that, I'm headed back to the city. But I managed to be here for all the excitement and this is just the opportunity I need. If

I get a story in to my editor before any of the others, it might just make the front page."

"Front page?"

Rackton could see the way the deputy leaned in and stared at him with intent eyes. Although he tried to sound casual, the deputy had already tipped his hand. Will was hooked.

"Oh sure," Rackton said. "A bank robbery in broad daylight. A roaring gun battle. And with a man like Clint Adams involved, I wouldn't be surprised if mine isn't the only paper interested."

"So why do you need to talk to the prisoners?" Will asked.

Rackton waved his hand dismissively. "Just for a few quotes. After that," he said, going in closer for the deal, "I'll want to talk to you. Maybe take down a firsthand account. You *were* there weren't you?"

The sides of Will's mouth twitched and he was just barely able to keep from smiling. "Yes, I was. Nearly got shot."

"Oooo. That makes for excellent copy. I'll definitely want to talk to you after I get this initial interview out of the way. In fact, would you mind helping me out a bit?"

"Oh, I don't know if I—"

"If you could just write down what you saw and did . . . just a rough guideline . . . it would ease my workload considerably." Leaning in and lowering his voice even though there wasn't anyone else in the office, he added, "I can make sure your name shows up prominently in the finished article. Maybe even above the sheriff's."

Will pretended to think it over for a few moments, although the only thing going through his mind was the best way he could tell Emma at the Cat's Eye Saloon that he was a famous man. He could already see the excited look on her face as he feigned his uncertainty to the man in front of him.

". . . I don't know . . . ," Will said. "I guess I can let you in, but only for a bit. And you'll have to leave that here," he said, pointing to Rackton's walking stick.

"Certainly."

"I need to make sure you're not carrying any weapons."

Rackton opened his coat and let the deputy quickly frisk him. Having dropped off his double shoulder rig before going to the sheriff's office, he let the deputy search all he wanted. When he was done, Will took the cane and set it on top of the sheriff's desk.

"They might be sleeping," Will said. "The prisoners, I mean."

"Is that a problem?"

"Nah. Just don't take too long."

"Come get me the moment you're done writing down your account. That way, I can get started writing my story as quickly as possible." When he saw some reservations creeping into the deputy's eyes, Rackton added, "Be sure to put in all the details of the battle. Otherwise, they might get left out of the story."

EIGHTEEN

Will busied himself by mentally listing every last detail he could remember. As he led Rackton out of the office and to the small jailhouse, the deputy listened to the other man talk about deadlines, editing and all kinds of other such nonsense. And once they were inside, the deputy pounded his fist upon the nearest bar. The rattling sound reverberated within the solid walls and rattled the brains of the three men laying either on their cots or against the wall of their cell.

"Rise and shine, assholes," the lawman shouted. As he moved toward the back of the narrow walkway between the cells, he kept banging against the bars, rattling the doors and making any other noise he could manage. "You got a visitor."

"Fuck him," Ben snarled before spitting a juicy wad toward the deputy's boot.

Will stopped and looked down at the glob that had missed him by less than an inch. His hand dropped down to the gun at his hip and he took half a step toward the cell before stopping again like a dog who'd suddenly run out of leash. "If I didn't have this badge, I swear I'd finish the job I started."

Ben didn't so much as twitch. Even when the deputy looked like he was about to draw, Ben stared straight back at him without blinking. "Shut your hole and get out so we can sleep."

Even though he knew he hadn't scared the prisoners in the least, Will kept up his bravado for the reporter's benefit. "This here is a reporter from a newspaper in New York City. Tell him what he wants to know."

"Why should we give a damn about any reporter?" one of the other prisoners asked.

This time, Will did move forward and plucked the gun from his holster. "You'll do what I say or I'll put a bullet through your head."

More irritated than cowed, the prisoner looked away and held his tongue.

That seemed to be more than enough for Will to feel good about himself once again. Turning to Rackton, he said, "I'll leave the door open so I can see you from the office. Will this take long?"

Rackton shook his head. "Not at all, Deputy."

"Good. I'll get started on that list you wanted."

"Thank you so very much."

Will nodded and shot another glare toward the prisoners. Pleased that none of the bank robbers had anything else to say to him, the deputy turned around and strutted out. It only took him a few seconds to get back to the sheriff's office, since the jailhouse was practically in that building's backyard.

Rackton watched the deputy until Will had gone into the office. True to his word, both doors between the jail and the sheriff's desk were left open as Will went back to his chair and gathered up a pencil and a small stack of papers. The lawman hunkered down over his writing like an eager schoolboy, glancing up at the jail every few seconds or so.

"And just who the fuck are you again?" Ben asked.

Turning so that his back was to the deputy, Rackton stared straight down into the bank robber's eyes and said, "I'm here to make you an offer."

"Is that a fact? And why should I listen to anything you got to say?"

"Because we have a lot more in common than you might realize."

NINETEEN

Although none of the men sitting at the table seemed to disagree with the arrival of Anne Kielly, her presence did slow the game up a bit. Everyone needed some time to feel the new player out, which stunted the easygoing flow that had been built up between Clint, Sam, Emmett and Billy.

Even so, the mood at the table was still just as enjoyable as it had been before. The rest of the players knew Anne well enough for them to joke around and treat her with some degree of respect. Acting as one player to another, Sam made a point to let Clint know that Anne wasn't someone that needed to be watched.

He didn't say so out loud, of course. It was communicated more through the occasional nod or offhanded comment at the right times. Clint didn't have any problem following Sam's lead. After all, he didn't have any reason to object to her being there. Women at a card game were a rarity and always made for some interesting plays. And since this particular woman seemed to already have been accepted by these local players, Clint was looking forward to whatever twists and turns might come.

Anne was dressed in a plain tan dress that laced up the

front. The top several laces were hanging loosely open to reveal her firm, rounded breasts. Her skin was smooth and seemed to have a golden hue that only made her hair seem that much more lustrous. The dress hugged her body nicely, displaying a trim hourglass figure.

Her blond hair was cut just above her shoulders, causing the ends to turn outward like feathers brushing against her neck. Like most beautiful women, she knew how to handle herself so that all the men around her had no choice but to be affected by the sight of her. Even Clint had to admire the way she used that asset to her favor. After less than an hour of play, she'd already managed to nearly double her money.

"How come nobody warned me you were a cardsharp?" Clint asked with a wry grin.

Patting the top of a stack of her chips, Anne grinned and replied, "Ladies are supposed to be lucky, Clint. I'm sure you'll get your chance to show me what you've got."

When she said that, she bit down slightly on her full bottom lip. That, combined with the turn of her eyes and the subtle lilt in her voice, sent a wave of heat through Clint's body.

"Besides," she went on. "Most of these came from Baby Face over there on that last hand."

Everyone at the table laughed at that one. Everyone, that is, except for Billy.

"Aw, Jesus," Billy groaned. "Now you all have her calling me that, too."

The more Emmett tried to hold himself back, the more his shoulders started to shake with the effort. Finally, he busted out laughing so hard that he had to take a moment to catch his breath. "I thought you'd learned not to try and bluff anymore, Baby Face. But with nothin' showing and just a pair of deuces in your hand?"

"Shut up, Emmett."

Leaning back in her chair, Anne seemed to be enjoying

the trouble she'd stirred up. Clint was amused by the exchange between Billy and Emmett, but he was more intrigued by the gorgeous blonde with the deep blue eyes.

It was Anne's turn to deal, and once she'd gathered up all the cards, she shuffled them and set them down to be cut. "Are you making fun of my card playing, Mr. Adams?"

Clint held up both hands and shook his head. "Not at all. In fact, I was hoping you'd take that as a compliment."

"I think you're the one just waiting to swoop down on me like some big ole hawk." She narrowed her eyes and cocked her head as though she was sizing him up. "You say a lot of things to get my defenses down . . . just so you can get me right where you want me."

Clint smiled and let a few moments pass. As she waited, Anne let her eyes drift down over his chest, the tips of her teeth pressing in ever so gently against her lower lip.

"Are you worried I might try to take advantage of you?" Clint asked.

Anne looked around the table. For the moment, Emmett had Sam distracted with his and Billy's continued verbal sparring. The bartender was coming over to refill the drinks, keeping the rest distracted even more.

Leaning in so that she could whisper to Clint, Anne said, "Don't get too full of yourself, cowboy. I might still be the one to take advantage of you."

Clint could smell the clean, vaguely flowery scent of Anne's hair. Her skin had a musky smell of its own that stirred something deep inside of him. Despite all that had happened with the last woman he'd been with, Clint couldn't deny that he liked the sound of what this one was saying.

TWENTY

"So just what the hell are you trying to say?"

Still sitting with his back against the wall of his cell, Ben looked at Mark Rackton as though the other man had just been scraped off the bottom of his boot. His fat body hung over the side of his cot, nearly hiding the cell's single piece of furniture completely under his considerable bulk.

If Rackton was put off in the slightest by what the bank robber had said, he didn't give the first clue. "I thought I'd made myself rather clear."

"You said we had something in common. What could I have in common with some lily-white dandy like you?"

Ben's men chuckled at their leader's comment while keeping their eyes fixed on every move that Rackton made.

"We're in the same line of business, first of all." Rackton paused and made a show of looking around at his cramped, dirty surroundings. "Although I don't think I'd be out of line in saying that I'm slightly better at my job then you are at yours."

Ben let out a single, disgusted breath before shifting

upon the creaking cot and closing his eyes. "Fuck you, whoever you are."

"That's the thing, Mr. Scott. You don't know who I am. But more importantly, you don't know what I can do for you."

Opening his eyes just enough for him to look out from beneath the puffy lids, Ben said, "Unless you plan on breaking me out of here, you can't do a whole hell of a lot."

"Breaking you out is only the beginning."

That caused Ben's eyes to snap open. He straightened up on the cot and took another, more careful look at the other man. "What kind of work are you in?"

"Ahh," Rackton said while stepping closer to the bars. He clasped his hands in front of him. The gesture made him look like a teacher or even some kind of strangely dressed priest. "Now you take an interest in what I have to say. Good thing, too, because I doubt that deputy will be kept busy for too long."

"You ain't no reporter."

"That's right. My name is Mark Rackton."

Furrowing his brow, Ben slid off the cot and got to his feet. Both of his men stood up as well, getting as close to the other man as the bars would allow.

"Mark Rackton?" Ben asked. "The one who knocked over the Union Pacific payroll office six years ago without firing a shot?"

In response to that, Rackton merely lowered his chin in a single, slow nod.

The man standing at Ben's side looked between his boss and the well-dressed visitor. When nobody else said anything right away, he spoke up. "He could walk in here and say he's Jesse James. For all we know, you're just some crackpot local who wants to look like a big man."

"Right," Rackton said in a slow, crackling voice. "With you men cooling your heels in those cages, if I wanted to look bigger than you, I wouldn't have to make up much of a story. Besides, Jesse James is dead. And after what you pulled, it won't be long before you follow him straight into hell."

Rackton fixed the prisoner who'd spoken up with a stare that was more than enough to back him down into the corner of his cell. Shifting his eyes back onto Ben, he said, "I'm also the same Mark Rackton that hunted down an entire posse last fall in the Dakotas."

Ben nodded. "I heard about that. Why'd you do such a thing?"

"Because I don't like being followed."

"All right. So what if you are Rackton? So what if you are a thief and a killer? So . . . what?"

"Our occupation isn't all we have in common," Rackton said. "There's something a little more recent that interests me. It's something that might just work to both of our advantage."

"I'm not much in the mood for any more guessing games, so why not do me a favor and spit it out."

"Clint Adams. I believe you've just recently been introduced to the gentleman?"

Just hearing that name was enough to drain some of the color from Ben's face. The other two bank robbers looked as though they were just about to climb out of their skins.

Rackton watched their reactions with no small amount of amusement. He didn't let that show on his face, however, since the prisoners were just starting to hang on his words. "I see that you feel about him in much the same was as I. That's good."

"How do you know Adams?" Ben snarled.

"Let's just say that he and I have some unfinished business."

"I'll need more than that."

Rackton didn't even try to keep himself from smiling

this time. Instead, he shook his head and regarded the bank robber with the same expression he might give to a cripple who'd just threatened to kick his ass. "Really, Mr. Scott. You shouldn't try to drag this out any longer. You're not exactly in an enviable bargaining position."

"If it wasn't for Adams, me and my men would not only be out of here and rich, but a few of them would still be alive. I may not like him, but I have to respect a man who can fight like that. Going up against him the wrong way might not be any better than swinging from a noose. At least here I know when the end's coming."

Rackton let out a breath. By the time he'd emptied all the air from his lungs, every bit of amusement on his face was gone as well. Like a bobcat that had unsheathed its claws, his entire manner had become darker and deadlier. His voice sliced through the air like an arrow.

"He put an end to my career," Rackton said in something close to a hiss. "He nearly put an end to my life. I want him dead and I want you to help me do it. I have a plan, and at the very least, he'll never be heard from again."

Regarding the other man with careful suspicion, Ben asked, "And if I help you, you'll get us out of this jail?"

Once again, Rackton gave one slow nod in reply.

"Then count us in."

TWENTY-ONE

Clint and Anne sat alone at the table.

Anxious for the chance to get up and stretch their legs, the other players were scattered around the saloon either drinking or swapping stories with some of the other regulars.

Anne sat with her elbows resting on the table and her body angled slightly down so that Clint could get a good look at her ample cleavage. Now that the others had gone, she acted much more affectionately toward him and rarely took her eyes away from Clint's.

"I've got a confession to make," she said softly.

"If you tell me you've been cheating, I might just have to shoot you."

Clint managed to keep a straight face for all of two seconds before breaking into a grin. She smiled as well, but he kept watching her all the same.

"Actually, I wanted to confess that I've been trying to hunt you down for a while now."

"Should I be worried?"

"Only if you're afraid of this." After saying that, Anne leaned forward and reached out with one hand to touch Clint on the side of the face. With the gentlest of pressure, she pulled him closer so she could kiss him softly on the lips.

Her touch sent chills through Clint's body and her lips were delicate and sweet. Anne lingered there for what felt like an hour, yet when she finally broke away, it felt way too soon. Before separating from him completely, she sucked on Clint's lower lip just enough for him to feel it, giving him one last bit of erotic sensation.

Clint had to catch his breath when she was finished. As he did so, the rest of the saloon seemed to fade away, leaving nobody but him and Anne staring at each other across the table. Her clean, natural scent swirled around and through him, making it harder for him to concentrate on anything else.

Once he finally did come back to his senses, Clint nearly dropped back against his seat and let the rest of the sights and sounds come back into focus. In the back of his mind, he still had a part that was warning him about what had happened with Natalia.

But even though he'd learned to be more cautious, he wasn't about to let one conniving liar spoil the rest of his nights.

"What are you thinking about?" Anne asked.

"I'm just wondering how long you've been hunting."

She smiled and sat back as well. "Longer than you think, obviously." Staring into his eyes, she held his gaze for a few seconds before asking, "You don't remember me?"

Hearing that, Clint studied her a bit harder, paying more attention to the exact details rather than the exquisite beauty of her features. He was just about to ask for a hint when something was triggered in his head. It was a memory that came through only vaguely. Clint felt like he was trying to read the date on a coin that was sitting at the bottom of a lake. Right when he thought he could make something out, it rippled into obscurity.

Then it hit him.

Or rather . . . they hit him.

It was her eyes. Those sparkling, alert, mischievous blue eyes which always made him wonder what trouble was brewing behind them.

"Wait a second," Clint said as he snapped his fingers. "Anne. Anne Robins!"

She nodded and bowed her head slightly like a magician who'd just produced the card that had been selected by someone from the audience. "That's me."

"Good lord, how long has it been?"

"Has to be going on three years now."

Now when Clint looked at her, he saw a whole other set of details. One of the first things he noticed was that she was considerably slimmer. But since Clint knew better than to comment on anything like that, he said, "You cut your hair. It was so long back when I saw you last."

Running her fingers through it while tilting her head, she suddenly seemed more self-conscious. "Yes, I cut it short when I left Maryland. I thought I'd get a fresh start here and this was something I could change right away. It's so much easier this way."

"And that's not all you changed Miss *Kielly*."

"Kielly is my maiden name."

Suddenly, Clint felt his stomach bunch up in the middle. "What? That means you were married when we . . ."

Anne smiled and laughed a little at Clint's discomfort. Reaching out, she patted the top of his hand and said, "No. I was a widow, just like I told you. And when we . . ." After trailing off in the exact way that Clint had done, she smiled a little wider. "That was the best thing that happened to me in a time when I thought there wouldn't be any more good times. After you left, I picked myself up and decided to keep making my own good times.

"I didn't have anything left in Maryland, so I packed

up and moved out. It's like you showed me there was still more life to live and a whole big world out there to live it in. I started using my maiden name again as a way to start over. Ever since then, I've been hoping to find you . . . so I could thank you."

After meeting so many people in those three years, Clint was happy he hadn't forgotten about Anne. Everything about their last night together was coming back to him like a welcome flood. At that moment, he realized just how well his instincts had been serving him. From the moment she'd sat down next to him, despite all the suspicions he'd been carrying around, he felt like he could relax his guard around her.

Clint also realized something else, which came out of his mouth before he even knew it. "I missed you, Anne."

When she smiled, all the warmth he'd been seeing before intensified. She leaned forward again and placed both hands on either side of his face. This time, their kiss was even more passionate. Their lips brushed together as they savored the feel of one another. Then, their tongues reached out and met . . . softly. The kiss quickly became more intense as they both struggled to taste more and more of each other.

Finally, they moved away from each other to catch their breath.

"I missed you, too," she whispered.

TWENTY-TWO

"So when do we get out of here?"

Rackton glanced over his shoulder and found the deputy glancing right back at him through the open doors. He then turned back around and held both hands in front of him. "Calm down. I'll get you out of here in a minute."

The robber next to Ben jumped forward and grabbed hold of the bars desperately. "Either we get out of here or we ain't doing anything else, you understand? Get us out now."

"Shut yer goddamn mouth, Henry," Ben snarled. "If you're gonna act like a little kid throwing a fit you won't be any use to us."

"Thank you," Rackton said as he looked back in the deputy's direction.

"Don't thank me for nothing. You do your part and I'll do mine. But I'll tell you one thing . . . if you don't do your part pretty damn quick, I might as well just go right back to sleep."

"I know you're feeling tense right now. That's why I waited to come here until everything I could put into place has been situated. But once you're out, you've got to do exactly what I say. Otherwise—"

Locking eyes with the man on the other side of the bars, Ben looked at Rackton with a primal ferocity that revealed a savage, almost animal nature within him. "Otherwise what? You'll kill us? Turn us back in to the law? You'd best not make any threats unless you're ready to back them up, because I got no more patience and nothing left to lose."

Rackton met Ben's eyes with his own. Instead of anger or a violent temper flaring within him, Rackton's eyes gave away nothing. No emotion. No violence. Not even a sign of life. Ben might as well have tried to threaten a dead man.

Only these dead eyes weren't completely empty. They reflected the cold promise of the grave as well as a long, hard road leading to it.

"Save that shit for someone who's scared of you," Rackton said in a calm, quiet tone. "That deputy is on his way at this moment, so you'd better make your decision now. Either work with me and get what we both want, or work against me and get enough pain to make you dream fondly about swinging from the end of that noose."

Nobody said a word inside that jailhouse. The only noise that could be heard was the footsteps of the approaching deputy.

Looking away first and nodding subtly, Ben took a few steps back toward his cot. "All right," he said. "Get us out of here and we do things your way. But the moment I see you're leading us wrong . . ."

"I would expect you to head out on your own," Rackton finished. "Just make sure we part company on friendly terms, because I can be a most unfriendly person to those that cross me."

"Fair enough."

As if on cue, the deputy burst into the jailhouse. Compared to Rackton's light, almost catlike footsteps, the lawman seemed to be pounding around like a sick elephant.

"These boys giving you any trouble?" the deputy asked.

Rackton shook his head. "No, sir. Thank you for coming, though. They were getting a bit rowdy."

Once again, Will took on the mannerisms of a triumphant hero as he kicked the bars with his right foot. Turning to glare at Ben, he shouted, "What did I tell you, lard ass? I said behave yourself or you'd have to deal with m—"

The deputy's threat was cut short as his head twisted to one side and his voice turned into a muffled grunt. Will's eyes blinked in disbelief, staring up at the ceiling as his hands started flailing about at his side.

Even the men in the cells were taken by surprise. All three of them flinched when the deputy's face moved back into its normal position, only to snap once again violently to the side. There was a wet, grinding *crunch* followed by Will's final, wheezing exhale.

His hand still instinctually flailing for his gun, Will twitched like a hooked fish as his body went through a set of spastic convulsions. His boots rattled against the floor, making it obvious that the only thing holding him up at all was Rackton's hands beneath his chin and on the back of his skull.

Once the convulsions settled, Rackton let Will drop and bent down to pluck the keys from his belt.

"Holy shit," Henry muttered from Ben's cell. ". . . H-holy shit!"

Rackton was already busy fitting keys into the cell door's lock, turning and trying again until he found the right one. On the third try, the lock clicked and the door swung open.

Ben stepped out, looked at the deputy's body and said, "He's not the only one around, you know."

"Yeah," Rackton said as he moved over to the other cell and started trying keys in that door. "I know. The other one went out for some food, leaving this one alone for a bit."

As soon as Henry was outside the cell, he ran to the jailhouse door and assumed a lookout position. "There ain't nobody out there."

"Not yet," Ben said, taking the gun from Will's holster. "But there will be. This was messy, Rackton. I thought you worked better then this."

Rackton turned the key and let the last bank robber out. "This whole town's messy. The sheriff was so concerned about giving the vigilantes a free shot at you that he didn't think to put more than one or two men on guard duty at a time. I guess he thought that since Clint Adams was still in town, he could just let him keep the peace."

At the mention of that name, Ben spat on the floor. He hit the deputy this time, splattering a juicy spot right on Will's head. "Adams is still in town?"

"Yes, he is." Rackton glanced both ways before walking out of the jailhouse and heading for the sheriff's office. The three bank robbers went with him, and when they got into the other building, they all headed straight for the gun cabinet.

"This was messy," Ben repeated as he helped himself to a .38 pistol as well as a Spencer rifle. "Adams will probably be coming after us."

Having already slipped his shoulder rig on, Rackton found his cane and tapped it against the floor. "This was supposed to be messy," he said with a grin.

TWENTY-THREE

The door came flying inward and slammed against the wall with a jarring rattle that was almost strong enough to loosen a hinge or two. It came swinging back toward the jamb and was stopped by the man who was crossing the threshold.

Clint's hands were full as he stepped backward into the room. Using his hip to keep the door from blocking his way, he wrapped his arms tightly around Anne's waist and lifted her up off her feet. He then swung her around so that she was inside his room and shut the door behind him.

Her eyes wide after having been swept off her feet, Anne giggled as though she'd been sneaking kisses behind her father's woodshed. "You almost broke the door," she said.

"Guess I got a little carried away," Clint answered. He didn't take his eyes off of Anne. Instead, he stared at her hungrily while sliding his hands once more over her generous curves.

"I think I was the one that got carried away." Pausing, Anne looked around. "Good lord, this is a nice room."

Clint's face was pressed against the base of her neck,

kissing her up along her ear and then back down to her shoulder. "Really? I haven't even been in it yet."

She was about to say something else, but Clint reached a spot that caused her to stop short and take a long, deep breath. Closing her eyes and leaning back, Anne let him have his way for a little while before breaking the silence again. "Even the ceiling looks fancy!"

That was just far enough away from what Clint had been expecting to hear that it caused him to stop what he was doing to see what she meant. As soon as he looked at something other than Anne, he was taken in by the same things that had caught her eye.

"Good lord," Clint repeated when he'd taken a quick glance around the room. "You weren't kidding, were you?"

She certainly wasn't. Although Phil had told him that he was going to give Clint the best suite in the hotel, he hadn't prepared him for just how deluxe the accommodations would be. To start, the room was easily triple the size of the room Clint had had when he'd first checked in. There was a sitting area near one of the two large windows looking down on Cedar Street, a small dressing area next to a polished oak wardrobe and a bed that was bigger than some of Clint's campsites.

There were beautiful paintings on the walls, curtains made of deep red velvet and a carpet in the middle of the room that practically begged to be experienced with bare feet. And when Clint looked up, he saw what else Anne had been talking about. The ceiling was decorated with a raised pattern of looping swirls, accented with flecks of gold paint to make it look like a pale sunrise within the room's four walls.

Even after Clint had looked at the whole room, he had to look at it all again. Anne was already darting from place to place, looking closely at every last detail.

"Jesus," Clint muttered. "If I'd have known the suite

looked like this, I would have been the one buying all of Phil's drinks."

"How much does this cost?" Under the circumstances, Anne's question didn't seem awkward in the least.

Clint shook his head while running his fingers over the smooth, luxurious bed curtains. "He didn't charge me anything extra."

When she turned to him, Anne's eyes were wide and she nodded in approval. "Looks like you got one hell of a deal."

"I know. I'll have to start running into a few more bank robberies so I can keep traveling in style."

Anne smiled at him from where she was standing by the window. Outlined in the shimmering moonlight, her hair seemed to have its own radiance. Her skin looked smoother than the silk sheets on the bed. "You look like you forgot why you came up here."

Making a straight line for her, Clint walked past all the room's finery and didn't stop until he was close enough to hold Anne in his arms. "Believe me, I didn't forget why I came up here."

"Oh," she said with a pout that made her mouth look even sexier. "I was looking forward to reminding you."

"Reminding me about what?"

Anne smiled and reached up to start unbuttoning Clint's shirt. While doing that, she kissed him once on the mouth and then kissed him on the chin. She kept working her way down as her fingers pulled apart his shirt. She kissed him on the neck and then down over his chest after she'd used both hands to pull his shirt completely off of him.

Letting out a deep, satisfied breath, Clint let her lips and hands wander all over him as she savored every inch that she could reach. Her mouth felt soft and warm as she pressed it against his skin. Her hands worked quickly and urgently, as if she simply couldn't get him out of his clothes fast enough.

Her lips brushed over his midsection just as she unfastened his pants. From there, she lowered herself down onto her knees, sliding Clint's jeans down over his legs.

By now, she was starting to use her tongue, gently flicking it in and out, teasing him by gently licking his skin. When she had him naked in front of her, she ran her hands back up over his body, raking her nails over his thighs, reaching up, and then trailing them down his stomach.

When he looked down at her, Clint saw that Anne was already looking back up at him. "I think it's starting to come back to me," he said.

"Oh, is it now?" Keeping her eyes focused on his, Anne reached her hand between his legs so she could slide her fingers along the length of his shaft. "Are you sure you don't want any more reminding?"

"I'm definitely remembering how much you liked to torture me."

Her smile came back and she licked her upper lip to make it even better. "Is this torture?" she asked. Her mouth was close enough to him that Clint could feel her breath against the sensitive skin of his penis.

Anne parted her lips wide and moved her head forward, placing her mouth around the tip of his cock without actually making any contact. Slowly . . . ever so slowly . . . she rubbed her lips around his erection while exhaling.

Pulling her head back, she looked up at him again and asked, "What about that? Was that torture?"

Clint wanted to say that it was. But on the other hand, he didn't want to say anything that might make her stop what she was doing. Instead, he slipped his fingers through her hair and urged her to take him into her mouth one more time.

Although she knew exactly what he wanted, Anne didn't move forward. Instead, she leaned back and closed

her eyes; gently stroking his cock while savoring the feel
of his hands running through her hair.

"Do you want me, Clint?" she asked.

"Yes."

Once again, Anne moved her head forward and held
her mouth open slightly. Still looking up at him, she
moved her lips over his penis, opened her mouth and then
took him inside. Once she had nearly all of him in her
mouth, she closed her lips around him, pressed her tongue
against his hard column of flesh and moved her head
slowly back.

When she whispered, Anne was close enough for her
words to feel like a heated breath against Clint's sensitive
skin. "Do you want me bad?"

"Yes."

"Now you know how I've felt since the day you left."
And without another word, Anne wrapped her lips around
him and gave him exactly what he wanted.

TWENTY-FOUR

"Do you really think Adams is coming?"

Rackton was keeping watch at the window of the sheriff's office while the bank robbers rooted around for their possessions along with any guns they could carry. "Oh, he'll be coming all right. I can guarantee it."

"Well, I can guarantee the sheriff will be coming, too, and unless that's another part of your plan, I'd suggest we skin out of here."

"My thoughts exactly," Rackton said. "Are you and your men ready to go?"

Each of the robbers had not only his own weapons, but a few from the sheriff's gun cabinet as well. They had rifles, shotguns and pockets full of enough shells to hold off an army.

"We're ready," Henry said.

The other bank robber nodded as well.

Ben was peering through a different window as he let out a low whistle. "Not a moment too soon, either. The sheriff's headed this way."

All of the bank robbers stepped away from the windows and doors, readying their weapons as they took up positions around the room. They didn't try to hide themselves completely, although they did a good job of keeping themselves out of immediate sight.

Ben moved into a shadow close to the back door. Henry crouched behind the desk and the third man flattened his back against the wall next to the front door.

As for Rackton, he straightened his jacket so that it hung smartly over his body. His shoulder holster all but disappeared beneath the finely tailored creases. The sheriff's footsteps could be heard climbing the stairs in front of the office as Rackton placed both hands atop his cane and cleared his throat like an actor waiting for his cue.

The door swung open, coming less than an inch from pressing against the face of the robber who was standing against the wall. Sheriff Durrey stopped on the threshold, his eyes darting to and fro as he took in the room before him.

"Who are you?" he asked once his eyes settled upon Rackton.

Rackton smiled nervously and said, "Don't mind me, Sheriff. I was just waiting for your deputy. I was talking to him about some business."

Sheriff Durrey stepped into the office and pushed the door shut without taking his eyes from the man he'd found in his office. "Where'd Will go, anyway?" he asked. "I told that damn kid not to leave—" Durrey stopped talking and dropped his hand toward the gun at his side when he spotted Ben's bulky figure standing cloaked in shadow.

Before the sheriff could clear leather, Rackton was already so close that he eclipsed his view of everything else. Rackton's cold blue eyes filled Durrey's sight and the only thing he could feel was the press of steel against his stomach.

Durrey's guts filled with hot, molten fire. The sound of a muffled shot roared through his ears, quickly followed by another shot from behind.

The second bullet ripped through Durrey's spine, ricocheted off of bone and lodged itself in a rib. Unable to think straight through all the pain, Durrey let his gun slip through his fingers and felt his knees buckle beneath him. Strangely enough, however, he couldn't seem to fall down.

Rackton still had his eyes focused on the sheriff's face. One hand was shoving a pistol into the lawman's gut while he had ahold of Durrey's shirt with the other. After thumbing back the hammer, Rackton pumped one more shot into the sheriff before letting him drop to the floor.

Once Durrey's body fell, Rackton could see the bank robber who'd been standing behind the front door sighting down the barrel of a rifle. The weapon was still smoking.

When the robber saw the expression on Rackton's face, his first impulse was to cringe back and point the rifle at him.

"What the fuck are you trying to do?" Rackton seethed. "I said we needed to get out of here before these bodies were found." He didn't even seem to concern himself with the rifle pointed at him as he raised his ivory-handled pistol. "You'd better hope you didn't call down any more of them deputies or you'll be the first one dead."

Ben stepped forward. He put a surprisingly calm hand on Rackton's arm and pushed it down slowly. "There ain't nobody coming. Is there, Henry?"

Henry was already back at the lookout. "Not yet," he said.

After pulling in a deep breath, Rackton nodded and holstered his gun. "Then let's get out of here. I've got a place for us to hide out."

"Then what?" Ben asked.

"I'll tell you when we get there."

TWENTY-FIVE

The bed in Clint's room was so luxurious that when he lay down on it, he felt as though he could forget about everything else beyond the suite's four exquisite walls. Silk sheets pressed against his back as Anne crawled on top of him.

She pressed her nails against his skin as she moved over him, arching her back like a cat until she could straddle his hips. Spreading her legs open just a little more, she fit him inside of her and lowered herself all the way down.

Clint let out a satisfied moan as his entire penis was enveloped by Anne's warm wetness. She moved her hips back and forth just a little bit until she found the spot that brought the smile back onto her face. Once there, she stayed still while rubbing the palms of her hands over Clint's chest, rolling her head languidly from side to side.

Her skin felt smoother than the silk sheets as Clint eased his hands over her thighs and up along her torso. He especially loved the way her nipples grew hard and taut right before his hands got to them, as though her body was anxious to feel his touch. Cupping her breasts, Clint squeezed them gently at first, but found by the noises she made that she wanted him to let himself go a little further.

Straightening her back, she clamped both hands over Clint's and held them right where they were as she began lifting herself up and lowering herself down in a slow, sensuous rhythm. Anne rode him slowly at first. When she felt his hands close tightly upon her, she leaned forward and put her hands on Clint's chest so she could slide his cock into her even faster.

Clint savored the feel of being inside of her and couldn't get enough of watching her naked body strain with the effort of making love to him, but that just wasn't enough. A surge of raw energy pulsed through him, making him take hold of her and roll her onto her back with him kneeling between her legs.

Anne looked up at him with renewed excitement, her eyes wide and her mouth open as if she was about to say something. But no words came out. Instead, when Clint slid his cock inside of her and thrust his hips forward, Anne could only cry out with ecstasy while grabbing onto the mattress with both hands.

It felt as though Clint had been waiting to take her for years. Every time he pumped into her, he felt an explosion of sensation that coursed through his flesh and instantly left him wanting more. He looked down at Anne spread out before him, her nipples pink and erect and her breasts swaying with the motion of her body.

Anne clenched her teeth and suppressed a breath, her nails digging deeply into the mattress. Her muscles tensed and her mouth opened wide, but only a strained groan came out. Finally, she let out her breath along with a wailing cry as a powerful orgasm rocked through her entire system.

Just watching her was almost enough to drive Clint over the edge. He grabbed hold of her firm, rounded hips and lifted her slightly off the bed. From that angle, he could thrust even deeper inside, which only drew out Anne's cry even longer.

Taking a breath, her body covered in a thin sheen of perspiration, Anne used her feet to push away from Clint, forcing him to disengage. Before he could ask what she was doing, Anne got onto her hands and knees, facing away from Clint.

It took a bit of control, but Clint had to take a moment before entering her again. He just had to look at the sight of her beautiful, firm buttocks raised slightly with her legs spread, offering herself to him. Clint ran his hands over her back and let the tip of his penis brush between her legs and slide along her pink, moist lips.

"How about I torture you for a change?" he asked while brushing his hands along the sides of her breasts.

Anne clawed at her pillow and pushed back against him. "Don't you dare," she whispered. "Get inside me now, or I'll—"

"You'll what?" Clint asked. He reached around with one hand to rub down her stomach. He kept reaching lower along her body, not stopping until his fingertip grazed against the sensitive nub of her clitoris. "You'll leave? You'll get dressed and go home?"

"Oh God," she purred. "Just . . . ohh . . ." But once she felt his fingers making slow circles over her clitoris, Anne couldn't concentrate enough to speak. All she could do was press her face against the pillow and moan as she quickly approached a second climax.

Right when he could feel her muscles tensing and her breath coming in quick, shallow bursts, Clint pressed down on her sensitive flesh and listened to Anne call out his name. The moment her voice started to taper off, he let himself do what he'd been dying to this whole time.

He moved his cock between her legs once again, causing Anne to instantly lift her hips for him. Clint then thrust inside of her, easing his entire length into her.

"Oh yes," Anne moaned as she felt Clint's hands take hold of her hips. "Oh God, Clint, yes."

Hearing her voice and feeling her pussy envelop him, Clint pulled out all of his stops and pumped into her from behind with all the strength he could find. The harder he pounded into her, the more Anne groaned with delight. She even started pushing herself back in time to his thrusts, until their bodies were coming together hard enough to shake the giant bed they shared.

Clint pounded into her one last time before his own climax swept through him. Exploding in a burst of sensation, he was immediately grateful for the overly large bed when he dropped over onto his side without even coming close to falling out.

It took a moment or two, but he finally caught his breath. When he opened his eyes again, he found Anne laying right beside him.

"Now that," he said breathlessly, "was worth waiting a couple years for."

Nuzzling up against him, Anne ran her fingertips over Clint's chest and said, "Maybe. But if you think you're going to wait that long again, you've got one hell of a surprise coming."

TWENTY-SIX

Once they were a mile outside of town, the group of four horsemen came to a stop for the first time since they'd climbed into their saddles. The lingering sound of thundering hooves still filled their ears and was now mixed with the deep, rumbling of the horses' breaths.

Behind the riders, Willett slept with only a few flickering lights showing through the darkness. Ahead were the Adirondack Mountains, looming like oppressive giants stooping down to scoop them up in their rocky hands. The moonlight bathed rock and dirt with a pale glow which turned into a luminescent sparkle as it hit Big Moose Lake off to the southwest.

Rackton was in front of the small pack of horsemen. He'd been the one to signal for them to stop and it was he who the others looked to for their next set of instructions.

"There's a shack less than a mile up the trail this way," Rackton said, pointing toward the mountains. "The trail forks off into some bushes. It's narrow, so you'll have to walk and lead your horses through until you reach the shack."

Ben craned his neck as though he thought he had a

chance of spotting the shack from where he was. "There'll be a posse coming for us anytime now. Shouldn't we get hidden a little better than that?"

"If you're not looking for it, there's no way anyone could find where the trail forks. I marked the spot with a strip of material tied to a stake in the ground." Rackton injected sarcasm into his voice like venom into a snakebite when he added, "Be sure to pull up the stake when you get there."

The entire time, Henry had been fidgeting relentlessly. His palms were sweating through his gloves and he couldn't seem to find a comfortable spot on top of the horse Rackton had provided. "I don't like this, Ben. We got lucky getting out of that jail and we got to keep riding. Maybe go until we hit Canada."

"Please," Rackton sneered. "Would I go through all that trouble just to get you recaptured now?"

Ben nodded. "Suck it up, Henry. Rackton's in this as deep as we are," he said while locking eyes with the well-dressed man. "Deeper, even. Especially since he was the one that killed them law dogs and broke us out. Ain't that right?"

As always, Rackton's voice was cool and calm. "You are correct."

Henry still didn't look appeased. If anything, he seemed to be even more worried now than ever. "Ain't nothing comes for free, Ben. What's his stake in all of this? What does he get out of us being free and all?"

"Now's not the time," Rackton said. "If you want to try your luck with heading north, then be my guest. I'm sure there'll be posses out all over the place looking for you. Especially since one of those deputies saw me right before I came in to fetch you three."

Hearing that, all of the bank robbers fixed their complete attention upon Rackton.

"What was that?" Ben asked.

"We didn't get all the deputies, you know," Rackton said with as much emotion as he might show discussing the weather. "Some of them saw me heading toward the sheriff's office. Some locals probably saw me, too. They'll know to come find me. And before you get too many big ideas, killing me won't be the answer to your problems either."

Henry was hunkered down in his saddle as though he was afraid of getting thrown into next week. In a tense, ragged voice, he asked, "Why not?"

"Because I have other partners involved with this. And if they don't hear from me soon, they'll tell the deputies exactly where to look and exactly how you men helped me execute those peace officers."

"Bullshit," Ben grunted.

Glancing confidently from one man to another, Rackton smirked ever so slightly and said, "Are you ready to take that chance?"

His eyes narrowing and his grip tightening around his pistol, Henry looked as though he was about to give his answer to that question in lead.

Rackton stood with his arms folded across his chest. As he studied the nervous bank robber, his hands opened and slid a little bit closer to his guns. The move was nearly imperceptible, but it was all he needed to make him confident he could get the drop on Henry if the moment became too much for the other man to bear.

"We don't need to fight," Ben said once he knew that Henry actually might draw. "Right now we need to get off this road and hole up someplace. This cabin sounds as good as anywhere else." Before Henry could object, Ben added, "And if it doesn't look good when we get there, we can move on."

"All right," Rackton said. "That sounds fair enough to me."

"You're damn right it does," Ben snarled. "I may not

be the most trusting soul in the world, but I know how to repay my debts. Since I'd rather be on the run then inside that damn cage, I'd say that I owe you a debt, Rackton. We all do."

Sitting on top of their horses, breathing in the fresh air and looking at the mountains splayed out before them, neither of the other two bank robbers could say much to object to Ben's last statement. Even Henry seemed to calm down a bit and nodded wearily when Ben looked to him for acknowledgment.

Without wasting another breath on the matter, Rackton turned his horse back toward town and snapped the reins. The animal charged into the shadows in a flurry of hooves pounding against hard, mountainous ground.

"I don't like it," Henry said. "Ain't nothing for free in this world. You know that just as much as I do."

Ben nodded. "I know. But we should be all right. Any trackers are gonna have a bitch of a time with this ground since most of it's rock. And it sounds like we won't be here for very long. Besides," he added while heading along the trail toward the mountains, "if we're going after Adams, this jailbreak sure as hell won't be free."

TWENTY-SEVEN

Despite everything that had happened throughout the course of this night, Mark Rackton couldn't help but feel good about the way things were going. Despite the smell of burnt gunpowder, which still clung to his clothes and the blood that was on his hands, he considered the evening to be more than just a success.

It had been more than he'd planned.

It had been downright satisfying.

As Willett drew closer and his horse galloped tirelessly while churning his legs with the sound of powerful drums, the gunman smiled to himself. The bank robbers were giving him a little more trouble than he'd expected, but overall they seemed to be falling neatly into line. They were, after all, much like predatory animals.

Always fighting for superiority within their pack and always having to assert themselves by baring their fangs and growling whenever they felt it was necessary. Looking back on it as he rode, Rackton figured he shouldn't have expected any less.

Let them growl, he figured. Let them bark and snap all they wanted, just so long as they wound up doing what they were told and going where he pointed them.

It didn't matter how big the dog was as long as he knew how to heel.

The lights inside some of the windows were getting closer. In fact, Rackton was almost able to make out some motion within some of those buildings when he pulled back on the reins. Once the horse's steps slowed down enough for the noise to blend easier into the night's regular sounds, he steered it toward the southern end of Willett.

Before long, he could hear some of the sounds coming from one of the local saloons. After the bluff he'd pulled off a couple minutes ago, Rackton thought he owed it to himself to stop in at the nearest card table and double whatever money he could get his hands on.

There was no other partner waiting to hear from him, although that wouldn't have been a bad idea. What kept Rackton's mind at ease was his certainty that, if push came to shove, he would be able to dispense with all three of the bank robbers and pin the lawmen's death on them.

He might not have been on his way to meet up with any nameless cohorts, but that didn't mean Rackton didn't have business in Willett. On the contrary, he had some very important business indeed.

The next step in his plan was ready to be taken and Rackton was more than anxious to see it through.

Unlike what he'd told to Henry, Rackton had been very careful when he'd approached Sheriff Durrey's office. The only pairs of eyes that saw more than a vague outline in the darkness were either in a bird's head or closed forever.

That being the case, when he turned his horse onto Third Street, Rackton held his head high and nodded politely to the few people he passed. It was late enough that most folks were either in bed or headed home. The saloons were still doing a fair amount of business, but nobody there seemed to give a damn who rode by so long as they didn't take a shot at them.

Judging by the looks on their faces and the overall quiet that still hung in the air, nobody had found the bodies of the lawmen in the sheriff's office yet. There weren't any voices raised in alarm or even any footsteps hurrying along the boardwalk, which suited Rackton just fine.

In fact, if the deaths remained undiscovered long enough, Rackton figured he might just have time for that card game after all.

The thought of playing a game of poker after the night he'd had held a certain undeniable appeal to the gunman. When he reined his horse to a stop in front of the saloon and wrapped its reins to the hitching post, Rackton patted his pockets and took a mental note of how much money was in his possession.

There wasn't enough to make a fortune, but there was certainly enough to buy a few drinks. For the moment, that was all he needed.

The first thing he did when he walked inside was look in the back where the card tables were set up. Although the rest of the town seemed to be sleeping, those that were awake appeared to be packed inside this place. Out of all the games in progress, there were only a handful of empty chairs available. After scanning the crowd once, Rackton clenched his teeth and looked over the place again.

"What can I get for ya, mister?" the barkeep asked as he leaned forward over the wooden countertop.

Rackton forced an easygoing smile onto his face and stepped up to the bar. "Maybe you can help me. I'm looking for a man."

"Who might that be?"

"Clint Adams. He's—"

The bartender cut him off with a raised hand and a quick shake of his head. "You can stop right there, mister. He was in here not too long ago, but he stepped out."

"Do you know when he'll be back?"

Leaning on his elbow, the bartender winked and said,

"After seeing the looks of the woman he was with, I'd say he won't be back anytime soon."

Suddenly, a deep, grizzled voice cut in on their conversation. "You talking about Adams, Pete?"

"Yeah," the barkeep replied. "You know where he went? This man's looking for him."

Sam took a moment to size Rackton up with a slow stare. "Whole damn town's looking for him. Who might you be?"

Rackton did his best to keep his contempt from showing. Considering what was going through his mind at the moment, it wasn't an easy task. "I'm a reporter from New York City," he said, deciding it was easier to fall back on a lie he'd already thought out. "I'd sure like to—"

"Jesus Christ," Sam groaned. "Just have a drink and let the man get his fun in peace. After today, I'd say he deserved it."

Rackton knew the woman who'd been talking to Clint. He'd even kept close enough watch on them to pick out the others who'd been sitting in at that card game within the crowded saloon. He didn't, however, think that Clint and Anne would slip away so quickly.

"All right, then," Rackton said. "It has been a long day, so I guess I'll get some peace and quiet myself."

As he turned and headed out of the saloon, Rackton could feel the older man's eyes burning two holes in the back of his head.

TWENTY-EIGHT

Clint sat on the edge of his bed with his feet hanging over the side. Behind him, the colossal mattress seemed to stretch out for miles, making the fact that there were only two of them on it even more glaring. Anne crept up behind him, draping one hand on his shoulder while lazily tracing a line down his back.

"What's the matter, Clint? Is something wrong?"

Savoring the feel of her nails gently scraping his skin, Clint reached up and covered her other hand with his own. "Nothing's wrong. I just feel a little . . . anxious, I guess."

Leaning her head on his other shoulder, Anne smiled. "I'm surprised you have enough energy to feel anything but tired."

"Actually . . . so am I."

"Then why don't you lay down and relax. I'll make you forget about anything that might bother you and soon you won't have the strength to sit up, not to mention feel anxious about anything."

In the back of Clint's mind, he was thinking about the last time he'd felt anxious for no readily apparent reason. It hadn't been that long ago and had ended up in a gun battle that would probably be talked about in Willett for several years to come.

After letting that roll around in his mind for a bit, Clint thought that some of that excitement still hadn't worn off. In fact, it was getting hard for him to believe that all this had happened over the course of a day. Letting out a calming breath, he stood up and walked across the room.

"I think I just need to get some fresh air," Clint said while gathering up his clothes. After pulling on his pants, he turned around and looked at Anne.

She was kneeling on the bed right where he'd left her. The moonlight washed over her skin, causing the shadows to accentuate every one of her curves. Looking back at him, she smiled and started to move forward, her breasts swaying slightly as she went.

That was all Clint needed to feel a stirring inside of him, as every part of his body urged him to stay in that room. Well . . . some parts more than others.

Returning her smile, Clint started buttoning his shirt. "I'll be back soon."

"You're still leaving?" she asked with a trace of genuine disappointment. "But I thought we could . . ."

"I know. I was thinking the same thing. And if I stay here another moment, I won't be leaving for quite a while. All I need is some fresh air and a little bit of time to myself. I'll be back before you know it."

Anne studied his face, looking for any reason she should worry about him. Part of her thought back to the last time he'd left, but that was nothing similar to this. Even then, he'd told her that he was leaving for good. Anne might have concerned herself with any other man taking the first chance he could find to run out on her.

But Clint Adams wasn't just any other man. He'd never lied to her. Even now, his eyes looked honest enough. The closer she looked, the more she could see a weary look inside of them, but that only went along with what he'd just said. Finally, she nodded and slipped back under the sheets.

"All right," Anne said. "You have had one hell of a day. Take your walk and I'll be here waiting for you. I can rub your back and we can get some sleep. That is . . . if you want—"

He stopped her by pressing a finger to her lips. "That sounds great, Anne. I'm looking forward to it."

Snuggling down into the luxurious bed, Anne put her head on the pillow and watched him throw on the rest of his clothes. After strapping on his gun belt, Clint left the room and didn't look back.

As much as he tried to put it aside, that same anxious feeling still nagged at the back of Clint's mind. The feeling itself didn't strike him as all that strange, since he'd learned to pay special attention to such things over the years. What bothered him was that he'd found that feelings like those were so rarely ever wrong.

The hotel was quiet at this time of night. Even the noises drifting in from the saloon across the street were nothing more than a distant hum of voices and the trickle of piano music. Phil was standing behind the desk and lifted his head when he saw Clint come down the stairs.

"Evening, Mr. Adams."

Clint walked up to the desk and offered his hand. "That's one hell of a room, Phil. You've got to let me pay something extra for it."

"Oh no. I couldn't have any of that. Although . . ." His face screwed up a little around the edges, as though he'd just bitten into a bad apple. "I hate to even bring this up, but there is a man coming in from the city tomorrow. He's an investor and—"

"Say no more," Clint interrupted. "I'll be out of there in the morning. Although, I may sleep a little late if that's okay. Is noon early enough?"

Phil nodded. The sour look on his face had been wiped

clean away. "That would be fine, Mr. Adams. Thanks for understanding."

Clint turned and walked across the lobby. Opening the front door, his eyes snapped immediately to what was laying on the boardwalk like some hastily dropped package.

"Oh my God," Clint said as he rushed outside.

The shape looked like a large bundle that had been spread out upon the boards. But Clint knew it was no simple bundle. After all, bundles didn't wear boots and a hat.

In just a few steps, Clint made it to the figure laying in front of the hotel. He reached down to turn the figure over, his eyes already picking out some familiar details about the clothing and general build. All he had to see was the side of the man's face to know his suspicions had been correct.

"Jesus Christ," Clint said when he saw the crushed facial bones and nasty, bloody gouge across the man's sunken cheek. "Sam! What happened?"

The older man opened his eyes and tried to say something, only to spit out a thick mass of blood.

Clint was working to get Sam onto his back when he heard someone else walking up behind him. Turning to look over his shoulder, Clint saw something coming at his face and moved his head less than a second before he felt a blunt pain, followed by a sharp, blinding ache.

TWENTY-NINE

The old man had been following him.

Rackton knew that the moment he'd stepped out of the saloon and taken a moment to adjust his coat. He made it a habit to constantly be aware of every sound and voice around him. It wasn't any type of sixth sense or anything, just a skill picked up after years of being on the run. In fact, Rackton's senses were so finely tuned that he could normally avoid trouble before it was right on top of him. That's how he'd been able to start walking about relatively carefree.

That old man had been looking at him funny the moment Rackton had started asking about Clint Adams. It had been a nuisance at first, but those footsteps came right behind him as he left the saloon. They were the same footsteps Rackton had heard right before the old man had started grousing to him about leaving Adams alone.

When he heard that he was being followed, Rackton let the steps get a little closer before walking across the street toward the hotel.

The footsteps followed him . . . just as he thought they would.

Rackton walked a little farther and paused just a split

second to listen for those familiar, oafish steps. They hadn't missed a beat and were still coming at him. With that being the case, Rackton stepped up onto the board-walk and walked to the hotel's door. The moment he heard those steps hit the wooden slats, Rackton turned on the balls of his feet and took a look behind him.

Sure enough, the old man was there. To his credit, he didn't seem too surprised that he'd been discovered.

"What's your business with—" was all Sam could get out of his mouth before the handle of Rackton's cane snapped straight up and out, catching him on the jaw.

Rackton had already sized up the other man back at the saloon and knew he couldn't rely on just that one shot to put him down. While Sam's head was still reeling back from the first blow, Rackton followed up with another, this time swinging the cane around and smashing in the left side of Sam's face.

Sam staggered to one side, but didn't drop. Instead, his hand went for the gun at his side.

"Do yourself a favor, old man," Rackton whispered while drawing the cane back for another swing. "Stay down while there's still a prayer of you getting up again."

But Sam didn't listen. Either that, or he couldn't hear what Rackton was saying over the rush of blood through his ears or the pain that flooded through his broken facial bones.

Rackton didn't wait to figure out which it was. He saw that the old man was still going for his gun, no matter how weakly, and let loose with another shot from his cane. The metal handle caught Sam in the temple this time, breaking the skin and sending a flow of blood rushing down his face.

For a second, Sam looked as though he was going to stay on his feet. But then he let out a shuddering breath and dropped to the boardwalk like something that had been thrown from a moving train.

Although he hadn't heard or seen anyone else around, Rackton took a quick look just to make sure that nobody had been watching what he'd done. Just as he'd thought, it was too late in the evening for there to be many people walking about and the street was relatively deserted. There were a few shapes farther down the block, but none that had been close enough to see much of anything in the darkness.

Rackton shifted his gaze up to the windows of the hotel. With everyone in town so anxious to talk about what had happened and what Adams had done, it hadn't been much of a problem finding out where the legendary Gunsmith was staying. After a little more snooping earlier in the day, Rackton had even figured out which room Adams was in.

When he looked up to check the windows, Rackton was surprised to see Clint Adams staring out through one of the larger windows on the third floor. That didn't fit with what he'd found out, which caused a knot to form in the pit of Rackton's stomach. To make matters worse, it looked as though Adams was about to look down at him at any moment.

Slowly, Rackton moved toward the front of the hotel, positioning himself in a spot that wouldn't be easy to see from where Adams was standing unless he pressed his face against the glass. Rackton was just about to pull Sam's unconscious body more into the shadows, but stopped himself before reaching out.

Surely Adams would be looking down at the street. And when he did, he would surely see the old man lying there like the pathetic bloody heap he was. Even if he didn't recognize the old man's face, someone like Adams couldn't keep himself from running down to see what had happened.

And when he did, Rackton would be there waiting.

It hadn't exactly been his plan, but Rackton wasn't

about to let an opportunity go by when it nearly dropped into his lap.

Taking a step out of the shadows, Rackton glanced up at that third-floor window. Adams wasn't there anymore. If he'd seen the old man laying there, he was on his way down in the next minute or so. Even less than that was more likely.

Pressing himself up against the front of the building, Rackton picked out a spot that was especially dark, where he could wait.

He didn't have to wait long.

With his ear against the wall, Rackton kept his eyes searching the street. It took a bit longer than he'd expected, but soon there were footsteps approaching the hotel's front door. Although he wasn't positive, Rackton's gut told him to be ready for whoever stepped out.

The door swung open, allowing light from inside to spill onto the boardwalk. A figure was outlined in shadow. "Oh my God," the figure muttered. It stepped forward, knelt beside the old man and spoke again. "Jesus Christ. Sam! What happened?"

Certain now that the figure was Clint Adams, Rackton moved out from where he'd been hiding and swung the cane toward the other man's head.

THIRTY

The cane's handle would have landed right on target if Clint hadn't moved. Rackton knew that Adams wouldn't be taken by surprise so easily, but he figured he had his perfect moment since Clint's hands were full with the old man's crumpled form.

In mid-swing, Rackton saw Clint turn around to look at him. He knew Adams would hear him coming. After all, the boardwalk hadn't been made for sneaking around. But Adams moved even faster than Rackton had figured. And his instincts were a little different than the gunman had imagined.

Rather than just turn around, Adams had been going for his gun as well. Although he didn't clear leather before the cane hit, Clint's body was moving defensively and the blow landed on hard bone rather than the soft spot Rackton had been aiming for.

Even more disappointing was the fact that the cane's iron handle didn't hit at all. Instead, it was the polished wooden shaft that struck Clint's skull, diminishing the impact significantly.

Less than a second had passed since he'd committed himself to the attack, but Rackton already knew he'd missed his chance for a perfect kill. But he didn't lose all hope.

Any type of kill would suffice.

Clint didn't want to let Sam drop back down onto the boards, but he wasn't about to ignore the warning from his screaming instincts, either. The moment he'd heard those footsteps coming from behind, Clint figured it for an ambush.

Whoever it was must have been waiting closer than he'd thought, because the knock to his head came before he could get much of a look at who'd delivered it.

Pain coursed through his head, dull at first but then turning into sharp, jolting spikes.

Clouds of dark red moved into the edges of his vision as the rest of the world started to tilt beneath his feet.

But Clint managed to catch himself before stumbling, and he used the pain as something to focus on while forcing his senses back to something close to normal clarity. In all, less than a couple seconds had gone by since he'd been hit, but Clint knew well enough that even half a second could mean the difference between life and death in some situations. This was most definitely one of those.

He shook his head one time to clear out the encroaching cobwebs and then lifted his Colt. By the time the pistol was at eye level, Clint was able to see straight down its barrel and aim in the direction from which that jarring blow had come.

All he could see behind him was empty space and shadows. The boardwalk thumped beneath him as quick footsteps moved just out of his field of vision. Clint twisted his body so he could set Sam down and pull his hand out from beneath his body in one motion. Continuing his turn, Clint jumped to his feet and did his best to steady himself.

Clint didn't think he was going to pass out, but his balance was still less than perfect. Pushing those concerns

to the back of his mind, he turned toward the hotel's door
and prepared himself for whatever might be coming next.
Those footsteps were starting to fade and the person making them was somehow managing to keep just out of
sight.

For a second, Clint wasn't sure where the steps were
headed. The pain in his head was making it hard to concentrate and it took all of his control to focus. After what
felt like an eternity, Clint realized the steps had gone back
inside the hotel.

That bit of certainty was something else for Clint to
focus on as he grabbed hold of the door's handle and
pulled it open. Rather than stand so he could look inside,
Clint moved along with the door itself, throwing his body
away from the opening while pivoting to the side.

The instant the door was more than halfway open, a
blast roared from inside the hotel. There were actually two
blasts, one following hot on the heels of the other, sending
dark smoke and hot lead into the air.

Clint could hear the bullets whip through the space
where he would have been standing if he hadn't thought
to clear the way. And as soon as the shots had been fired,
he slid along the wall and headed for the closest window
looking into the lobby.

"Sorry, Phil," Clint said as he used the handle of his
Colt to smash in the expensive smoked glass.

Jagged shards sliced into his arm as he moved to look
through the hole he'd created, but it wasn't anything se-
rious. Clint barely even felt a scratch as he stepped in
front of the window and sighted down the barrel of his
modified Colt.

He caught a fleeting glimpse of a man dressed in dark
clothes. Before he could make out any details, Clint
ducked back down when he saw a gun being pointed in
his direction.

One more shot was fired, but it went wild. Since he

was so close to the glass and the only available light was coming from the other side of the window, Clint could see the dark figure through the smoked pane. The figure was running toward the stairs as fast as he could, taking full advantage of the time his last shot had bought him.

Since the last thing he saw was that figure running up the stairs, Clint ran toward the door and charged inside the hotel. He looked around the lobby for any other attackers, but couldn't find a single living soul. Just then, he caught a hint of movement and turned to look as Phil poked his head up from behind the front desk.

"He went up the stairs," Phil said shakily.

The hotel's owner started to say something else, but Clint didn't stick around to hear it. Instead, he was already peeking around the corner to get a look up the staircase. "Are these the only stairs?" he asked.

"No, there's a set in back," Phil quickly answered. "Behind the kitchen."

Clint looked to the desk and saw where Phil was pointing. Going that way might have been the long route, but Clint figured it would be better than running straight into another ambush. Once again, the other man started to say something, but Clint was already charging through the dining room on his way to the set of double doors leading to the kitchen.

THIRTY-ONE

Clint bolted through the dining room and nearly tripped over a chair which he hadn't seen until he moved around one of the tables. The adrenaline pumping through his veins must have been strong enough to counteract the effects of the knock he'd taken to the head because he jumped over the chair and landed squarely on his feet. Although the floor teetered slightly beneath him, Clint ignored it and kept moving.

There was a set of double doors in the back of the dining room which Clint hoped led to the kitchen. Charging through them, he saw a pair of ovens as well as several tables lined up with cooking utensils, pots and pans. There was also a portly woman with a very surprised look on her face who froze like a rabbit that had just found itself in a wolf's sights.

Clint paused just long enough to get his bearings and spotted the set of narrow steps along one of the walls. Charging past the frightened woman, he took the steps two at a time as a shrill screaming filled the room behind him.

The staircase wasn't half as well maintained as the set in the lobby. In fact, there weren't even any lights lit inside the narrow passage, leaving Clint to his own instincts to judge how wide the stairs were and how they were spaced.

After a few stumbling attempts and near falls, he found a good stride and made his way to the second floor. The landing wasn't much more than a wide spot where his steps echoed slightly more than they had before. Clint felt along the wall at around waist level and came across a door handle pretty quickly.

He turned the handle and pressed his body against the door. Opening it slowly until he could just peek outside, Clint hoped that his steps hadn't been too loud and that he wasn't a split second away from catching some lead.

Knowing there was only one way to find out, Clint moved his head and glanced through the narrow opening. The door was at the end of the hall, giving him a clear view all the way down the second floor. At the far end of the hall, he could see the landing for the main stairs.

Crouching there, that same figure in dark clothes was laying in wait with his gun at the ready.

Clint was just about to make his move when the figure turned to look in his direction. Clint still couldn't see much detail in the dimly lit hall, but there was no mistaking the sight of the gun shifting to aim down toward his end.

This time, Clint had been expecting the worst and he didn't flinch when he saw the gun turning his way. Instead, he steeled himself and got ready to take a shot of his own. Pointing the Colt as though he was simply pointing his own finger, he drew a bead on the figure at the other end of the hall and squeezed the trigger.

The Colt went off a heartbeat before the dark figure's weapon. Both explosions rocked through the hall, to combine into one uneven blast. The bullets crossed through the air, hissing like deadly insects toward their targets.

Clint had figured the other man had been taken somewhat off his guard and pulled his trigger in haste. Such calculations burned through his mind, keeping him from ducking for cover. Fortunately, he was right and the incoming bullet drilled into the wall a few inches off its mark.

From where he was, Clint couldn't see if his own shot had hit, but before he could take another one, the figure was already on the move once again. The darkly clad man spun in a tight circle, making Clint think that he might have caught the Colt's round and been knocked off balance.

But rather than fall over, the figure rose up from his crouch and darted across the hall.

Clint wasn't about to just stand by and wait to see what happened next. Instead, he lowered his aim slightly and pulled the trigger again. The Colt bucked against his palm, spitting out another chunk of hot lead toward the other man.

This time, Clint knew where his bullet landed since he saw a dusty plume shoot out from the wall. Judging by the splinters that were fluttering through the air after having been chipped away from the wall, the bullet had only missed the figure's legs by an inch or less.

Before Clint could take another shot, the figure made it to the bottom of the next flight of stairs. Using the wall for cover, he poked his head around and took another shot.

Having lost the advantage of surprise, Clint pulled himself back into the cramped stairwell as the other man's gun went off down the hall. There was the sound of an impact near Clint's position, and a hole was punched through the wall less than a foot from his head. Despite the fact that he'd been on the receiving end of that one, Clint had to admit that it was a hell of a shot.

Even under fire and in a hurry, the other man had damn near put his target down. The only thing saving Clint's skull from getting another hole drilled through it was his instinct to seek cover.

But rather than stand there thinking about it, Clint was already running up the stairs to the third floor.

THIRTY-TWO

As his feet pounded up the stairs, Clint pictured the layout of the next floor. He compared what he'd seen from the last floor to what he already knew of the third so that he wouldn't have to waste valuable time getting his bearings. When he got to the next landing, Clint was ready to charge through the door, ready for anything.

Rather than waste time with the handle, he kept his momentum going at the top of the stairs and put his weight behind his shoulder. He didn't have to see the door in the darkness to know it was there, and the moment he made contact with something solid, he heard the welcome sounds of wood crunching into pieces.

The door flew open and Clint burst into the third-floor hallway. His Colt was at hip level and his finger was already tightening on the trigger as he looked for any sign of his target.

At first glance, the hall seemed to be empty.

But as he looked for anything out of the ordinary, Clint knew there wasn't any place for the figure to hide. Since his own suite was on this floor, he knew that the hall was nothing but a straight row of doors. The stairs were also out since the only place they went from here was back down.

Clint walked quickly down the hall, fighting back the urge to run. He'd just passed one set of doors when he noticed something out of the ordinary. It wasn't much, but it was more than enough to set his nerves on fire.

One of the doors farther down the hall was slightly open.

In fact . . . it was *his* door.

Thoughts of Anne filled his mind and he quickened his pace toward the familiar entrance. When he got closer, Clint kept his steps as quiet as possible without sacrificing any of his speed. Once there, he pressed his back to the wall next to his door and used the back of his heel to push it open the rest of the way.

In one smooth motion, he swiveled so that he was facing into his suite while dropping to one knee into a firing stance.

One shot immediately exploded from within the suite, cutting through the air where Clint's head would have been if he'd been standing up straight.

Clint's eyes darted straight to the puff of smoke inside the large room, using that to center in on the source of that last gunshot. He was just about to return fire when he saw a familiar face. Anne stared back at him with anxious fear, her eyes darting back and forth between Clint and the pistol being jammed up beneath her chin. Rackton stood behind her with one arm cinched around her midsection and his face peeking around from behind Anne's head.

"If you've got any feelings at all for this one," Rackton hissed, "I'd suggest you keep your distance. Otherwise, you'll be scraping her brains off the ceiling."

Clint didn't make any sudden moves toward the pair, but he didn't lower his gun either. "Who are you?" Clint asked. "One of the bank robbers?"

Rackton smiled. Only the corner of his mouth could be seen from behind his human shield. "Right. And I came all the way back here just to see what I could get out of your room."

"Then what are you doing here?"

Jabbing Anne's chin with the end of his gun, Rackton pushed her face to one side so that more of his face was unobstructed. "Take a look at me, Adams. See if it jogs anything loose in that head of yours."

Clint studied the other man's face. It seemed just as familiar as one of the town locals who he might have passed on his way to get breakfast. Then again, since he could also see frightened tears streaming down Anne's face, it was awful hard for him to concentrate.

"I'm not in the mood for games," Clint said. "How about letting the woman go so we can talk like men?"

Rackton shook his head. The expression on his face seemed like a snake's smile: cold and humorless. It was more the way his lips were cut than anything expressing emotion. "I've got a better plan. I want you to come in here and sit down in that chair over by the window."

Stepping all the way into the room, Clint started inching his way around Anne to get a clearer shot at the gunman, but Rackton moved with him. He twisted around, keeping Anne between himself and Clint.

Anne was too scared to talk. Anything she tried to say only came out as a shuddering sob.

"Shut up," Rackton growled. When he dug the gun in deeper, he saw Clint's body tense. "Go ahead and try it, Adams. You might get me before I pull the trigger. Of course, then I'll probably blow her head off anyway. A body has a way of clenching up when it dies. Trust me . . . I've seen it plenty of times."

"I'm real impressed," Clint said as he moved toward the chair. "Now are you going to tell me what this is about? Why did you hurt Sam like that? Who is he to you?"

"Sam?" Rackton asked. Finally, realization dawned on him as he kept turning until his back was to the door. "You mean that old man? He was merely a way to draw you out. I know you can never pass up the opportunity to play hero."

Clint kept his eyes glued onto the gunman. He watched every move and waited for any clear shot to present itself. But the other man seemed to know right when to step one way instead of another. He kept his head moving back and forth in an irregular pattern, keeping himself mostly hidden behind Anne's terrified face.

Rackton had started backing toward the door now, inching his way closer to the hall. "Nothing near you is safe anymore, Adams. That's what this little visit is all about. You need to know that you're not the hero you think you are . . . and you're certainly not the hero all these locals think you are.

"I'm going to come after you and chip away piece by piece. I've been watching you long enough to know plenty of nice, easy targets like this pretty little thing here."

Anne nearly collapsed when she heard that. Her body started to go limp, but Rackton held her on her feet within his iron grip. Tight, rope-like muscles drew in around her waist and the barrel of his gun kept her head up straight.

"You got something against me?" Clint asked. "You're not the only one. Let her go and we'll settle it."

"Nah," Rackton answered while shaking his head. "I've also watched you enough to know that going against you in a straight fight would be damn close to suicide."

"So you'd rather fight dirty? That's no way to even up any score. Whatever I did to you . . . it won't help to go around killing innocent people that have nothing to do with it." Clint was in front of the chair that Rackton had mentioned.

"Sit down," Rackton said. "And put the gun on the floor."

Clint did as he was told, setting the Colt down by his foot.

"Now kick it toward me."

"Let her go first."

After a moment, Rackton took his arm away from Anne's waist. "Kick over that gun and she'll walk away."

His mind racing, Clint tried desperately to come up with a way to keep Anne alive without giving this lunatic what he wanted. He knew better than to think that the gunman would stay true to his word. Unfortunately, Clint couldn't think of a way out of this that didn't put Anne at risk. At the most, he could buy her a couple more seconds.

When he sent the Colt sliding across the floor, Clint prayed that he'd be able to make those seconds count.

THIRTY-THREE

Rackton never thought that Adams would part with that fancy gun of his. In fact, he was beginning to think that he'd made a terrible mistake by not shooting the woman as a way to distract Adams long enough to put him down. But when Adams seemed to play along with his requests, Rackton decided to go with the flow of the situation until things got too far out of hand.

The Colt spun a couple times on its side after being kicked toward him. Although the pistol didn't make it all the way to him, it was far enough out of Adams's reach to keep the gunman satisfied for the moment. Even so, he kept backing toward the hallway.

"So what now?" Clint asked.

Rackton kept his eyes on the other man, keeping in mind all the things he knew about the Gunsmith and his knack for getting himself out of sticky situations. "Now you'll keep tight and stew for a bit."

"I thought you'd want to finish this thing. Or am I not at a big enough disadvantage already?"

"We'll finish this all right. But when it happens, you'll barely see it coming. Besides," Rackton added, "it's not any fun unless you get to let things roll around inside you for a while. Get you all nice and worried for a bit. That way, you'll get a good taste of what I went through."

"I don't even know who you are," Clint said. "How would I know what you went through?"

"Does this sound familiar? 'Next time I see you, I'll put you down. Count on that.' "

Clint shrugged. "I might have said something like that. But I could have said it to any number of people."

"That's your problem, Adams. You talk too much and you let too many folks go when you should have just put them down when you had the chance. Consider all of this a lesson. And everything that happens after tonight will teach you to mind your loose ends . . . because they might just be the death of you."

Keeping his body loose and his eyes on the gunman, Clint didn't concern himself with making any sense out of what Rackton was saying. There were bigger concerns to deal with at the moment and something very specific he was waiting for. That specific something was the whole reason he'd given up his Colt.

More importantly . . . that specific something looked as though it was just about to happen.

Rackton moved himself and Anne forward a step or two. Keeping his gun pressed against her back, he reached down for the Colt with a steady, outstretched hand. He watched Clint like a hawk, readying himself to blow the woman away the instant he saw Clint do anything he didn't like.

His hand touched against the bare floor. Rackton swept to either side, unable to make contact with the pistol. Out of sheer reflex, he dropped his eyes for half a second to see where the Colt had landed . . . which was exactly what Clint had been waiting for.

In a motion that was nearly too fast to see with the naked eye, Clint's hand dropped to his waistband where he'd stashed the .32 pistol that he'd taken from the bank robbery earlier that day. Up until a few minutes ago, he'd forgotten it had been there at all. But now that it was in his hand, Clint thumbed back the hammer, took quick aim, and fired.

THIRTY-FOUR

The gunshot sounded like a loud *pop* within the suite. Echoes from the shot had barely had a chance to form before Clint was surging forward to take hold of Anne's wrist.

Rackton spun in a tight spiral, his body thrown that way by the bullet which tore through his shoulder. The force of the impact hit him like a swing from a two-by-four, nearly sending him off balance. He barely realized he'd been hit before he thought to pull his own trigger.

Finger tensing with lethal purpose, Rackton fired even as his body still twisted around like a top. But not only was his aim wrenched off to the side, his target wasn't even in the same spot.

Anne didn't know what was going on. One moment the two men were talking, and the next there were guns going off and the world was turning crazily around her. At first, she thought she might have been hit. She was falling and felt a dull pain in her arm and shoulder. But then she saw Clint right next to her as though he'd suddenly appeared there with his hand wrapped tightly around her wrist.

The next thing she knew, the floor was rushing up and Anne was barely able to brace herself before knocking herself out on the boards. Another shot went off and the floor shook beneath her body.

Clint was about to take another shot with the .32 when Rackton squeezed his own trigger. Both guns barked inside the room, filling the air with smoky thunder. Looking at the woman on the floor beside him, Clint checked for any sign that she might be hurt. By the time he looked up, Rackton was gone.

"Are you all right?" he asked.

"I . . . I don't know," Anne stammered. "I think so."

The thought that she might be hurt was immediately followed in Clint's mind with the guilty feeling that any injury of hers would have been his own damn fault. He shouldn't have acted so quickly. She might have been killed. Instead of saying any of this, Clint took a moment to check her over.

He couldn't see any blood and she seemed to be moving well enough. "Stay here," Clint said as he jumped to his feet.

Keeping his head low, he bolted through the suite and made a straight line for the door. Along the way, he scooped up the Colt which was still on the floor right where he'd left it. After a quick toss, the .32 was in his left hand while the Colt took its place in his right.

Every one of Clint's senses was at its peak the closer he got to the hall. He could hear footsteps and voices, but it was hard to say by then which belonged to Rackton and which were just curious hotel guests poking around to see where all the shooting was coming from.

Clint tucked his head in close to his chest and rolled out through the door. He knew he would be a target the instant he came out of there if Rackton was waiting for him the way he had been at the stairs. The move wouldn't have won any awards, but it got him out of the room and to the other side of the hall in a rush.

Landing with his toe against the wall opposite his door,

Clint looked both ways with his Colt at the ready. There was nothing moving in the hall and no shots being fired at him. Without wasting another moment, Clint got to his feet and headed toward the stairs.

He got there without the dramatic flair he'd used to leave his room. For the most part, that was because everything in his head told him that such precautions were no longer necessary.

Just like any other animal with its back against the wall, Rackton was going to fight or flee. Since Clint didn't see any traces of another fight, he figured that the gunman had opted for the second of those two choices.

Just to be sure, he made his way carefully down the stairs, holding his Colt in front of him. There were other guests looking panicked and confused in the halls, but the fact that they were there at all told Clint that Rackton wasn't among them. The people he saw simply didn't look frightened enough for their lives to be in danger.

Clint made his way all the way down to the lobby, where Phil was just peeking up from behind the desk.

"He left," Phil said. Pointing toward the front door, the hotel owner added, "He went through there."

Clint looked outside. The only thing that caught his eye was Sam lying on the boardwalk. Although the older man had definitely seen better days, he seemed to be stirring. Other than that, the street was clear. Since Clint didn't know which way to run, he decided to go back and clean up the mess that the gunman had made.

"Son of a bitch," he grunted as he pounded his fist against the hotel in frustration. When he looked back at the front door, Clint spotted a young man placing a timid foot over the threshold. "Do you know where the doctor is?" Clint asked.

The other man seemed skittish at first, but quickly nodded when he got a look at Sam's bloody form.

"Then go get him," Clint commanded. "And get the sheriff while you're at it."

Clint wasn't about to wait for a response from the other man. He was satisfied enough when the guy took off running down the street. Phil stepped out next, moving straight for where Sam was laying.

The hotel owner knelt down and looked into Sam's face. "He's still breathing, thank the lord. Sam's a tough old bird. If he made it this far, he'll pull through just fine."

Clint heard the words, but he was already moving back inside. He figured Sam was in good hands for the moment, which freed him up to tend to something that nagged angrily at his mind. Taking the stairs two at a time, Clint bounded up to the third floor and nearly stormed into his suite.

At the sound of his approach, Anne started to dive behind the bed. When she saw who was coming, she stopped, froze and then threw herself into Clint's arms.

Questions poured out of her, but they came in such a rush that the words all blended together. Clint simply nodded, held her tightly and told her everything was going to be all right.

"It's over now," he whispered. "We're all right. It's over."

Although he was glad that she seemed to be taking some comfort from his reassurances, Clint didn't take any for himself.

This was a long way from being over, he knew. A long way, indeed.

THIRTY-FIVE

The shack that Rackton had found at the base of the Adirondacks was barely much more than four walls leaning against each other. The roof let in more wind and moonlight than it kept out and judging by the warped, rotting floor, it had even less luck with the rain. To say that the place was furnished would have been an insult to the term. The two chairs and single table could barely stand up on their own and were fairly teeming with hungry termites.

Ben hardly even noticed the state of the walls or furniture. He'd been keeping a post by the window ever since they'd arrived. Every noise in the darkness outside caught his attention. Every movement he saw was nearly met with a round of gunfire from one of his stolen weapons.

Sitting on the edge of one of the sturdier looking chairs, Henry was checking over the rest of the guns they'd taken from the sheriff's office. He was also counting every last round of ammunition. "I still say we skin out of here before morning," he grunted. "We've got enough ammunition to push back a posse, especially since we took out the sheriff and one of their deputies. By the time the others get their heads together, we could be drinking as free men in Canada."

Ben didn't take his eyes from the window as he replied, "Yeah, that sounds just great. Since we killed them law dogs, the price on our head will get even higher. And with Adams on our trail, that will just make things even worse."

"I never heard about Adams working for hire."

"Neither have I. But he does work with the law and I doubt he's the type to just ride away after what happened."

Henry thought that over for a moment or two as his hand closed around the rifle he'd picked out as his own. "That Rackton fella seems to have something against Adams. I say that's even more reason to cut out of here. The more I hear, the more I don't like any of it."

Ben tensed and lifted his pistol. Behind him, the man at the table jumped to his feet.

"What was that?" Henry asked.

After letting out the breath he'd been holding, Ben said, "Nothing. Just Anders walking by on lookout." Ben nodded to the last remaining member of his gang as he walked by. Anders nodded back and continued circling the cabin.

"I still haven't heard much of a reason why we're still here," Henry said. "Jailbreak or not, Rackton's crazy, we don't owe him—"

"We owe him plenty," Ben interrupted. "And like it or not, Adams will be after us. His type don't let a town's sheriff get gunned down without doing anything about it. Even if he doesn't ride after us right away, we'll have to be looking over our shoulders for him everywhere we go. I don't know about you, but that don't sound like any way to live."

Henry shook his head. "Adams won't come after us. Not for long, anyway."

"Are you ready to take that chance?"

The question didn't come from Ben. It came from the

back of the cabin, behind the table where Henry was sitting. The sound of the new voice startled Henry so much that he nearly fell out of his seat. Ben spun around and snapped the hammer of his pistol back with a quick, pudgy thumb.

Standing there, looking as though he'd just gotten back from a quick stroll through the woods, was Mark Rackton.

"Where the hell did you come from?" Ben snarled.

Rackton stepped inside through a back door which none of the bank robbers had even noticed. That section of the wall looked just as rickety as the rest and wasn't marked by so much as a single handle or visible hinge. As soon as Rackton closed it, the door seemed to melt away into the rest of the poorly maintained filth.

"I just came in from town," Rackton said. "Did you miss me?"

The robbers eased back somewhat, but still looked as though they were only a hair's breadth away from pulling their triggers.

Ben didn't turn away from the window. If anything, he looked through the dirty glass even more intently. "What'd you go back to town for? Are you trying to *make sure* that you were followed this time?"

"You're close," Rackton said. "I had to deliver a message. While I was there, I got the opportunity to pay Mr. Adams a little visit."

Henry looked as if he was about to crawl out of his skin. "You what?"

Rackton had yet to look the least bit concerned. He even managed to keep his composure as he absently rubbed the fresh wound on his shoulder. "It got a bit out of hand, but it served its purpose nonetheless."

THIRTY-SIX

"What message are you talking about?" Henry asked. "You owe us an explanation, dammit!"

After pausing just enough to settle himself into one of the chairs, Rackton fussed with the crude dressing he'd tied onto his wound. "You're right," he said, looking at Ben. "Looking over your shoulder isn't much of a way to spend your life. Trust me. I learned it the hard way five and a half years ago in a New Mexico cantina."

Neither of the robbers were about to say anything at the moment. Once Rackton saw that he had his audience right where he wanted them, he set one foot on top of the table and went on.

"It wasn't too long after a train job I pulled back then. Not a bad job, although it turned a little messy."

Ben looked away from the window and fixed his eyes upon Rackton. "Wait a second . . . are you talking about that Union Pacific that was derailed on its way from California?"

"Yes. That's the one."

"I heard about that job. In fact, that's the first time I ever heard your name." The fat man snorted and grinned in a way that made him look like an overly ripe pumpkin.

"A little messy, huh? Every man guarding that payroll wound up dead. Not to mention the twenty or so passengers that got shot. You made all the papers with that one."

In a sick, twisted kind of way, Rackton actually looked a little proud when he heard Ben say those things. "Like I said, it got messy, but nothing I couldn't live with. Anyway . . . I met up with Adams when I was on the run and there was some trouble in New Mexico.

"Me and one of my partners were stopping over for drinks when there was trouble at a cantina. Adams was there as well, but he must not have recognized us. That was, after all, before our likenesses were plastered on posters throughout the country." Once again, that proud expression drifted across his face.

"There was a fight," Rackton continued. "My partner got greedy and demanded a bigger share. The rest of my men were there as well, but we kept our distance so we didn't look too suspicious. I was teaching my partner the problem with greed when Clint Adams decided to poke his nose in where it didn't belong."

Rackton no longer looked proud. Instead, he stared intently at a point directly in front of him, ignoring the rest of the world. His voice dropped to a strained whisper which sliced through the air like a dull razor blade. "Adams outdrew me. Right in front of my men . . . in front of the whole damn cantina. I took the fight outside and nearly got the drop on him, but he was too fast.

"Too . . . damn . . . fast. He made me look like a fool, as though he was just trying to fill some time. He looked at me . . . over that fucking Colt . . . and told me to get out of town." Focusing once again on the men inside the cabin, Rackton laughed and said, "Like he was doing me some kind of favor. He made me look like a weak, pathetic fool in front of my own men and told me the next time he saw me, he'd put me down."

Once again, Rackton stared off into space as if he could

see the image of what had happened flickering in the air like some kind of shadow play. "There wasn't a sheriff in that town, so Adams took my gun and sent me on my way. The cantina owner bought him a drink and I never saw any of my men again. You know all the money you read about in them papers? I never saw a dime of it."

Rackton pulled in a breath that sounded like steam building up inside the belly of a train's engine. "I had to go by a different name after that. You know how word spreads among men like ourselves, I'm sure. Two of my men even came after me for some money I had from other jobs. They said I was weaker than they thought, so why should they let a scalded dog take off with their money.

"Of course . . . they said that right before I gutted them with this." Rackton snapped his wrist, plucking the handle off his cane to reveal a thin, gleaming blade about as long as his forearm. The blade sliced through the air with a metallic glimmer and in the next second it was gone. Rackton snapped the handle back into place and tapped the cane on the floor.

Ben glanced at something outside the window. His hand clenched around his pistol and his breath came up short, but eased up again when he saw Anders walk by in yet another sentry pattern. His nerves felt like bits of frayed twine inside his body. He no longer tried to hide the fact that every other sound made his pulse quicken or that every shadow caught his eye.

"Adams let you go," Ben said. "And for that, you want to go after him?"

Nodding slowly, Rackton circled the table and stepped around Henry's chair. Each step was marked by the tap of his cane against the floor. Each tap was just a little louder than the dark figure's own steps which seemed to be only muffled disturbances in the cabin's stagnant air.

When he got around the table, Rackton looked at Henry and nodded slightly. Turning back, Rackton's body snapped into motion like a cobra launching itself toward unsuspecting prey. The cane's handle snapped apart one more time and the thin blade sliced through the air.

Before he could do anything about it, Ben felt the cool press of steel against his throat. There was no pain. There was only a slight twinge at his throat, followed by the warm trickle of blood running down his neck.

The blade stayed right where it was, twisting ever so slightly between Rackton's fingers. "Don't like this too much, do you?" he asked. "What do you think your friend over there is thinking about? Do you think he sees you the same way as he did before I turned you into a helpless little dog?"

Although Ben knew better than to move any more than it took to breathe, he glared at the other man with an intensity that almost sent heat ripples through the air. His face turned deep red, which nearly matched the crimson stain growing at his collar.

Moving so that he could stare directly into both of Ben's eyes, Rackton spoke through tightly clenched teeth. "If I had to place a wager, I'd say that I'm not your favorite person right about now."

"You'd be right about that," Ben replied, even though it widened the gash on his neck.

"And if I did this in front of a whole town, putting this picture into your men's heads when your pockets were still fat after a big job, I'd say you'd like it even less."

Ben didn't have anything to say to that. The angry color in his face started to drain away, however, and his eyes lost a bit of their murderous glint.

Rackton eased back on the blade before pulling it completely away. "A man can steal all the money he needs, Mr. Scott. But once his pride is gone, it doesn't come back so easy. For a man to purposely take someone's pride from them is inexcusable. Trust me. I know. Clint Adams might have thought he was being the better man by letting me go, but he made me skulk away like a dog and I've been paying for it ever since."

"Fine," Ben said while wiping the blood from the slice at his neck. "You made your point. It would do all of us good to be known as the men that killed Clint Adams, but how does everything else fit into it?"

Henry had been on his feet from the moment Rackton put the knife to Ben's throat. Of course, he hadn't done much since then but try to look imposing. "Yeah," he said. "Why stay here after that jailbreak? All we're going to do is make it easy for Adams to find us. And what message did you deliver? You still never told us about that."

Once again, Rackton was back to his calm, collected self. "That's simple. We *want* Adams to find us now that we're here. And as for the message, that was just to make sure he wouldn't miss the fork off the trail to get here."

THIRTY-SEVEN

Clint lent a hand to carrying Sam from the front of the hotel to the doctor's office, which was three streets away. Actually, he lent his shoulder, his back and an arm to the effort since Sam insisted on going on his own two feet even though he could barely walk. With the help of another local, the job went fairly quickly, which allowed Clint to hurry back to the hotel.

Anne was waiting for him in the lobby. She'd thrown on a plain gray coat to match her equally dour expression. Sitting in a padded chair, she jumped up to meet him the instant she spotted Clint walking through the door.

"There you are," she said while wrapping her arms around him. "I was so worried about you."

Clint gave her a hug and said, "That's pretty brave talk considering you were closer to that killer's gun than I was."

"I was worried about you all the same. It seemed like he didn't even know that I was there."

Although Clint was sure Anne had come awful close to meeting her maker, he decided it was better to keep that to himself rather than worry her after the fact. Kissing

her gently on the lips seemed to calm her a little more. It
didn't do him any harm, either.

"Mr. Adams," a voice said from somewhere to Clint's
right. It was Phil. The hotel owner was holding something
in his hands and shifting restlessly on his feet. "I . . . uh . . .
meant to give you this earlier, but with all the commotion
it kind of got set aside."

"What is it?"

"A message. It's from the . . . uhhh . . . visitor who
came earlier. He tossed it down on his way out."

"You mean that bastard that nearly killed us?" Clint
asked in disbelief.

Phil nodded. As soon as he held out the piece of neatly
folded paper, it was snatched out of his hands.

In his haste, Clint almost tore the note to bits while
unfolding it. The words became visible slowly but surely
as the paper was straightened out to its full size. The script
was surprisingly ornate. Each letter was crafted in an el-
egant, swirling style that looked more like a theater pro-
gram instead of a note dropped by a killer on his way out
of town.

The more of it Clint read, the harder it was for him to
finish. His stomach tightened into an angry knot and it
was all he could do to keep from tearing the note into
confetti.

The note read:

I trust I have gained your attention by the time you
read this. I plan on picking at you like the scab that
you are, until one of us is dead. No more bloodshed
is necessary except for yours. Meet me to end this.
The longer you wait, the more I'll have to keep
picking.

                                        Mark Rackton

Suddenly, Clint remembered why that name had

been familiar. The last time he'd seen it was on a wanted poster along with a crude rendition of Rackton's face. It wasn't until he saw that name in print that he was finally able to make the connection. Now that he knew who he was dealing with, Clint shook his head and started crumpling up the note. He stopped, however, when he saw the map sketched onto the back.

"What does it say?" Anne asked.

"Nothing. Just an invitation, that's all."

"An invitation to what?"

"Something that I thought was over and done with years ago."

Anne shuddered at that, drawing away from Clint as though she thought the note in his hand might reach out and snap at her. "So you know who he is?"

Clint nodded. Despite all the anger that was going through him, he had to laugh. Doing so made him feel a little better, but didn't cool the heat that had been burning inside of him ever since he saw what that maniac did to Sam and Anne. "Yeah, I know him. But just barely. He was some robber who pulled a big job in New Mexico a while back. I ran into him in a cantina where he was shooting up the place over some squabble with his men.

"I didn't think much of it at the time. I didn't even really know who he was. All I knew was that he'd already hurt a bunch of people trying to do nothing but drink their drinks, and he was about to start shooting a bunch more. I took him outside, put him in his place and told him to start walking."

Anne looked at him, expecting the story to continue. When it didn't, she furrowed her brow and asked, "That's it?"

"Yeah. That's it. I never saw him after that, until I happened to spot one of his wanted posters in Albuquerque. The picture wasn't that great, but it was close enough. That's the first time I even knew what his name was. I didn't recognize it until just now when I saw it written down again."

"Well, there has to be something else. It sounds like he got off light if all you did was kick him out of a cantina."

After mulling it over for a couple seconds, Clint shrugged. "There may be more or there may not be," he said. "Some men like that don't even need a reason."

Anne looked down at the note and wrapped both arms tightly around herself. When Clint noticed her discomfort, he folded the paper up and stuffed it into his pocket. She smiled sheepishly, but seemed to be more at ease.

"Being that close to him, I could almost feel how much he wanted to hurt us," she said. "I don't know how, but there was something about him. Something . . . evil."

"Crazy's more like it, but I know what you mean. Whatever reason he has is important enough in his own mind. Rather than waste my time trying to figure it out, I'd rather make sure he can't hurt anyone else."

"How?"

"By finishing what he thinks I started," Clint said. "Only this time, I won't be so nice."

THIRTY-EIGHT

Despite all the courtesies Phil had shown him, Clint took Anne out of that hotel and to another place in town. The hotel owner understood completely and apologized as though he felt responsible for what had happened in and around his own place.

Rackton had gone to Clint's room as though he knew exactly where to look. He'd probably been following Clint for a while before making his move. The very thought of that started to heat Clint's blood again, but he got a grip on himself before he got too bothered.

The last thing Clint needed was to allow himself to be manipulated by some lunatic with a vendetta. In fact, Clint was certain that Rackton had done all of this just to get him mad enough to make a mistake or two. At least that much of what happened made sense.

Sam had been beaten down and left to bleed in front of Clint's hotel not too long after the older man's friendly card game.

When he had his chance at hitting Clint from cover of darkness, Rackton passed an opportunity for a killing blow.

And in the end, Rackton passed on every other room

inside that hotel so he could make a straight line for Clint's. Once there, he grabbed hold of Anne just so he could mess with someone that Clint might have cared about.

There was no more doubt in Clint's mind. Rackton had been purposely trying to goad him into losing his temper. The note, along with everything else, was just his way of stirring the pot until Clint was wrapped up tightly in rage.

It wasn't the most subtle of strategies or even the most complex, but it was a valid one all the same. There was a certain ruthlessness needed to deliberately hurt so many people just to provoke someone else. Most others would simply put a bullet in someone to make their point. In a sad, strange way, that was easier than sticking around to watch someone squirm or listen to him beg and scream.

Simple killers did just that. They killed.

Rackton wanted something else. Clint didn't have to know the other man to know that he wanted not only to kill him, but to hurt him as well. The fact that Rackton had followed him and watched for the best people nearby to target showed that Rackton was willing to take his time to get whatever revenge he desired.

Something else bothered Clint, however. Namely, the fact that he'd only just met Sam at the card game earlier that evening. And he didn't know Anne was in town until a few hours after that. And since Clint himself didn't have a master plan concerning his travels, that meant that un- less Rackton was phenomenally lucky, he must have been following Clint for some time and watching him in every town he'd been in.

The killer might have been following him for months . . . or even years . . . waiting for some combination of people or places that fit whatever his pattern might have been. That notion sent a cold feeling through Clint's bones. It wasn't fear, but more of a combination of anger and wea- riness.

Men trying to make names for themselves had been coming after him ever since he'd had a name of his own. Complete strangers wanted to kill him just for the sick honor of saying that they'd done it. Now there was one man who'd been shadowing him for God only knew how long like some twisted living ghost.

And now that this one had shown himself, Clint had to wonder if there were any more out there like Rackton. Perhaps this was the only one, or perhaps there was an entire legion out there following him.

Perhaps, perhaps, perhaps.

Too many of those and Clint knew he would make himself just as crazy as Rackton. So rather than think about it any more, he decided to only concern himself with the things he knew to be facts.

First of all, Rackton was out there and wanted Clint to come after him. That was the most reasonable purpose behind these attacks.

Second, Rackton wanted Clint to meet him at this spot shown on the back of the note he'd left. According to the map, the place was some cabin off the trail leading into the Adirondack Mountains. It looked like it would be hard to find without directions, which also meant it was a good place for an ambush.

Which was the third fact he could safely say for sure: This meeting was *definitely* a trap. A hidden meeting place in unfamiliar, mountainous terrain—hell, it might have come straight out of a textbook written on ambushes.

Fourth, Clint knew he had to ride straight into that cabin whether it was a trap or not. Rackton had made it plain that he would keep on hurting people until he settled this business with Clint. Too many people had been hurt already, and Clint would be damned if he was going to stand by and watch any more.

Better people than this lunatic had come after Clint, and there would be plenty more. That was a fact that Clint had learned to live with a long time ago. All he could do was live his life and deal with such men as they presented themselves. If Rackton wanted a fight, Clint would just have to give him one.

A fifth fact that settled firmly in Clint's mind was that Rackton knew his own limitations. That was something that could be used against him later when the time came.

For now, however, Clint decided to see about arranging for some backup in the fight that was coming. The town's sheriff seemed to have his heart in the right place, so Clint figured that the lawman would be more than happy to carve out a piece of Rackton's hide for himself. After all, the last thing Rackton might be expecting was to be denied his little war and just get thrown into a jail cell like any other criminal.

In fact, Clint was starting to like that idea more and more. It was the killer's rule that this fight be one-on-one, not his own. There didn't have to be anything written in any note for Clint to know that much. Besides, this was the law's problem, wasn't it? Let them worry about Rackton.

All of this had been going through Clint's mind as he made his way to the sheriff's office across town. He'd been on his way to see if Durrey had anything to offer that might be a help against Rackton and had just gotten within eyeshot of the office when he noticed something peculiar.

That particular word drifted through his mind like a familiar, yet unwelcome visitor. This time, however, the *peculiar* feeling was much stronger than when he'd noticed the fat man posted across the street from his hotel.

His concerns doubled when he saw the deputy come staggering out of the office. Clint broke into a run when the sharp scent of gunpowder reached his nose.

THIRTY-NINE

"... H-holy God ...," the deputy muttered as he stumbled out of the sheriff's office.

Clint took one look at the young man and knew it wouldn't do much good to try and talk to him. Besides, he didn't need someone to explain things to him when the entire picture was painted in blood right in front of his eyes.

The door to the office swung open, its hinges making a shrill squeak that reminded Clint of a distant scream. Even though the lighting was dim and flickering, he could make out enough gory details to cause the hairs on his arm to stand on end. Keeping his hand on his gun, Clint pushed the door open and stepped inside.

Sheriff Durrey's body lay sprawled out on the floor, his blood forming a thick pool all around him. The place had obviously been sacked. Every last cabinet had been opened and dumped, while every single desk drawer had been pulled.

Clint could feel his blood starting to boil again, but he forced himself to calm down. The best way for him to do so was to keep in mind that his getting angry was exactly what Rackton wanted. Thinking about that made Clint stop short and turn around.

"Where are the others?" he asked the deputy, who stood outside with his back to the door.

The younger lawman held his hands propped on both hips and was taking deep breaths. By the sound of it, he was fighting back the urge to vomit. Finally, he steeled himself enough to reply to Clint's question. "You mean the other deputies?"

"Yeah. Where are they?"

"I . . . I was the only other one besides Will, and he was keeping watch on the jailhouse."

Clint moved out of the office and took a quick look around. "Where's the jailhouse?"

Too close to losing the fight with his stomach, the deputy jabbed a trembling finger toward a smaller building behind the office. Clint jogged for that building just as wet, retching sounds erupted from the deputy behind him.

Covering the distance to the jailhouse in less than a second or two, Clint drew the modified Colt and headed for the front door. With the fears that were running through his mind, he knew better than to just charge on inside. Instead, he pressed his back against the wall next to the door and paused to listen for any noises coming from within.

It only took a quick glance for him to see that the jail's door was slightly ajar. Every window was barred and the latch on the door was not broken, which only made the fears inside Clint's mind grow even bigger.

Since he heard nothing coming from inside, Clint took a deep breath and used the back of his heel to kick open the front door. He waited a second for anything to come out, but there was only silence. Trying to keep some hope alive inside himself, Clint kept his head low and moved away from the wall to jump into the doorway.

He sighted down the barrel of the Colt as he looked

inside the jailhouse. The first thing he saw was the empty cells and open doors. From there, it just got worse as he spotted Will's dead, broken body laying on the floor with his head twisted at a grotesque angle.

In that instant, Clint's fears were realized. The knot in his stomach loosened somewhat now that he knew what had happened. Being right, however, didn't make him feel any better.

Suddenly, Clint heard the sound of something scraping against the floorboards behind him. In a blur of motion, he spun around and dropped to one knee as the Colt snapped up in preparation to fire.

The only thing Clint saw was the pale-faced deputy. His wide eyes were fixed upon the body on the floor, so much so that he didn't even seem to notice the gun pointed at him.

Clint quickly lowered the Colt and stood up. "When did this happen?" he asked the younger man.

The deputy didn't respond at first. His eyes were glazed over, but he managed to snap himself back into the present after rubbing his hands over his face. "I just found them a minute or two before you got there. I was supposed to relieve Will for guard duty and I saw . . ." His words trailed off and he started to slowly shake his head. "How did this happen? I thought all those robbers were rounded up. Who was left to break them out?"

But Clint knew the bank robbers weren't broken out of jail. By the looks of it, someone had opened the door and let them walk out. And since Clint wasn't a big believer in coincidences this big, he figured that Mark Rackton was the man who'd turned the key.

Clint didn't know exactly how the escape had been pulled off, but he was fairly certain that someone as crafty and intelligent as Rackton would be able to figure it out. That son of a bitch might have been crazy, but that didn't make him stupid. In fact, it took some brains to put a plan together and have it ready to go at a moment's notice.

Although he wouldn't say so to the deputy, Clint wasn't too horribly surprised that someone had gotten the drop on a small, relatively unsuspecting bunch of lawmen like these. Durrey seemed like a fine man, but he also seemed to be a little out of his league with the bank robbers. Rackton was obviously too much for him.

The deputy was looking at Clint as if he was waiting to receive his next set of orders. Clint had seen similar expressions in photographs of soldiers in the War Between the States. The deputy had that same dazed, overwhelmed stare as those soldiers. Except, unlike the men in those pictures, the deputy was already beginning to come out of his daze.

"What are we gonna do?" the lawman asked.

Clint knew what *he* was going to do. Unfortunately, the deputy had no part in it. "First of all," he said, "you need to gather up some volunteers to watch over things until you can get a new sheriff. There may not be any prisoners left, but that doesn't mean things are going to be quiet in their absence."

"Do you think they'll come back?"

"I couldn't tell you for sure. All I can say is that you need to be ready in case something does happen. At the very least, you'll need some men to keep things quiet in case there's anyone in town who might decide to take advantage of the situation."

"What situation?"

Clint wheeled around so that he was staring directly into the deputy's face. He took hold of the younger man's shoulders and held him still. "This is a hell of a terrible thing that happened," Clint barked. "But you're all that's left of the law here and you've got to keep doing your job. There's got to be some folks you can count on in this situation. Deputize them. Keep the peace. That's your job."

Startled at first, the deputy began nodding as his eyes lost their stunned glaze. "Yes, sir. You're right. But what about those men that escaped?"

"Let me worry about them. I have a feeling that I know where they're headed. If I'm wrong, then that means they're probably halfway to Canada by now. Either way . . . they're not your concern at the moment."

Wriggling out of Clint's grasp, the deputy started pacing the room and collecting his wits. "I can round up the Plager brothers. They'll help me for a while and they're not too bad with a gun. After that, I can find Emmett. I can count on him."

"Good," Clint said. "You do that. I'll check in with you tomorrow to let you know about those prisoners."

Sensing that the deputy was pulling himself together well enough, Clint turned and started jogging toward the livery.

"Wait!" the deputy called out behind him. "Mr. Adams!"

Clint stopped and turned around. "What?"

"I don't remember exactly how this goes, but you're . . . uhh . . . you're deputized."

Smiling, Clint nodded. "You're doing fine, kid. Keep it up."

FORTY

"Are you out of your mind?" Ben asked as he tore himself farther away from the window then he'd been in hours. "You actually told Adams where to find us?"

Henry got up so fast that he knocked over the chair behind him. It looked as though he was set to grab Rackton by the throat, but he was stopped in his tracks by a single warning glance from the dark figure. "What's the use of hiding out here if you just tell everyone where we are?" Turning to Ben, Henry said, "The law could be coming for us right now! There could be a posse on its way up that path any damn second."

"There won't be any law coming for us for some time," Rackton said.

Ben locked his eyes on the killer and spoke through clenched teeth. "Oh yeah? How can you be so goddamn sure about that?"

"Because we killed most of the law in Willett," Rackton answered. "All that's left is a deputy . . . maybe two . . . and they won't stop pissing themselves until we've pulled out of here."

Henry looked back and forth between Rackton and Ben. "And we'll be pulling out of here real soon, right?"

"No," Ben said evenly. "Because the law ain't our problem. We got someone else headed this way that could gun us down a hell of a lot quicker than the law. Ain't that right, Mark?"

Rackton nodded. "You could say that."

It took a few moments for Henry to pull his mind back on track, but when he finally did, he lost a bit of the color in his face. "Shit. Adams. He's on his way."

"Yeah, Henry. He is," Ben said. "And thanks to our friend here, we don't have any edge to use against him."

"We outnumber him four to one," Henry said hopefully.

Ben simply shook his head. "That won't be enough against Clint Adams. I heard he shot his way through ten men down in Little Rock. Surprise would've been nice, but we don't have that anymore. All because Rackton got his nose bent out of shape for something that happened years ago on the other side of the country."

If Rackton took offense to anything that was being said, he didn't show the first sign. Instead, he seemed to be enjoying the discomfort of the two bank robbers.

"You really are crazy," Ben said. "Now I know that for a fact."

"I'm crazy?" Rackton asked with a subtle grin. "Then ask yourself how I got up to this cabin without your man outside even hearing a single footstep. Or ask yourself how I got inside this cabin without either of you two knowing about it until it was too late. Did either one of you stop to think about that?"

Although Henry seemed too flustered to think straight, Ben was taking everything in and chewing the information like a piece of bone that still had some meat on it. Rackton saw all of this and wasn't at all surprised. Watching Henry out of the corner of his eye, he focused most of his attention onto Ben.

"Adams will find this place," Rackton said. "He's *supposed* to find this place. And even though he'll know I'm waiting for him, there's no way he can be ready for all that I've got up my sleeves."

FORTY-ONE

Ben squinted at the dark figure. "Like what?"

Backing away from the fat man, Rackton leaned against one of the cabin's rickety walls like he was genuinely proud of the squalid surroundings. "I've had my eye on Clint Adams for plenty of time. He moves around and I move with him. I spent my time watching what he does— where he sleeps, what he eats, the people he talks to, even the battles he chooses."

"And I suppose he never noticed you doing any of this?" Ben scoffed.

"Do you notice every single face in every single town you go to? When someone does look familiar, do you assume that he must be following you or do you just shrug and move on?" When the fat man didn't reply, Rackton nodded. "That's right. Clint Adams may be hell and Jesus with a pistol, but he's still a normal man living his life. And like any respectable thief, I'm fairly good at keeping myself out of sight.

"In all that time, I picked up enough about Adams that I started getting ready to take him on. I didn't have to watch many of his fights to know that I couldn't beat him in a straight shootout. Even with the numbers in my favor,

I couldn't be certain of surviving such an encounter. Therefore, I had to find some other ways to stack the odds in my favor."

Henry laughed once in a way that sounded like he was trying to clear the back of his throat. "That sounds real brave of you," he muttered.

Turning to lock eyes with Henry, Rackton stared as though he was trying to burn a hole clean through the other man's skull. "You want to trade lead with the Gunsmith . . . be my guest. My guess is that he'll drill three holes through you before you even get your thumb out of your ass. If you think anything different, say so right now."

Henry was angry enough to spit. He wanted nothing more than to reach out and knock Rackton right across the jaw. He didn't, however, say one word to shoot down the other man's challenge.

"Didn't think so," Rackton hissed.

Shifting between checking the window and looking at the other two, Ben spoke in a voice that was becoming tenser by the second. "Fine. So you don't want to face him head-on. What then?"

"What we do then," Rackton said, after turning away from Henry as though the other man simply no longer existed, "is get every possible factor on our side. I've already got knowledge of the way Adams works and fights. After that, I started scouting ahead for the perfect battleground to make my move. Every time he moved on, I went ahead to look for someplace to suit my needs. Once I found it, I began my preparations and tried to make my move."

"Just out of curiosity," Ben said. "How long have you been doing all of this?"

"Only the last year or so."

"And how many places have you set up?"

"Things never fell into place just right, or Adams was

gone before I was ready. I've never set a place up completely . . . until now."

Laughing sarcastically, Henry held out his arms and looked around at all the walls and furnishings that surrounded them. "You call this place complete? No wait . . . I'll bet you'd say this was perfect. This goddamn shack ain't good for anything but firewood, and if you say any different, I'll know for sure that you ain't got the sense God gave a mule."

"You're right about one thing," Rackton shot back. "This cabin is perfect." Holding up one hand, he ticked off his points one by one on his fingers. "It's secluded and hidden in uneven, rocky terrain, making it hard to track or be tracked . . . but you know that much already.

"I already memorized every important detail about this section of land and scouted out several perfect spots for sniper nests, ambushes, hiding places and watch points. I've even found two alternate routes for us to come and go as we please without being seen.

"Beyond this place, I made sure to get Clint Adams worked into such a lather that he couldn't possibly be at the top of his game," Rackton added proudly. "That jailbreak of mine not only freed you men to help me take down our common enemy, but it also wiped out most of the law dogs that could have hampered our hunt.

"And, as Henry so kindly pointed out, we still have the good old-fashioned edge of outnumbering Mr. Adams four to one. Combined with everything else, I'd say we stand a better than average chance of being the men who get to put an end to the Gunsmith's distinguished career."

For the next several moments, Ben was completely silent. Henry didn't say anything either, but he seemed to be waiting for the nod from his boss rather than contemplating anything original on his own. Finally, Ben let out a tired breath and stood nose-to-nose with Rackton.

"We're in this," the fat man said. "But mostly because

we don't have much choice. We owe you for getting us out of prison and covering our tracks afterward, but after this job's done, we part ways with no strings attached. The slate's wiped clean. Deal?"

Rackton nodded and extended a hand. "That's a deal."

FORTY-TWO

Eclipse ran like a bolt of lightning out of town. All Clint had to do was touch his heels to the Darley Arabian's sides and the stallion was off. Grateful for the chance to stretch his legs after being cooped up indoors for the last day, Eclipse charged down the trail and headed straight for the mountains, his powerful lungs filling with crisp air in gusts.

It was plain to see that Rackton had been purposely digging at Clint's emotions, trying to draw him into some kind of trap. Clint knew where the trap was, who was behind it and what Rackton was capable of. That was going to have to be enough to see him through the ambush planned for him, since Clint wasn't about to sit back and let Rackton hurt anybody else just to get at him.

Although he couldn't prove it, Clint's gut told him that Rackton was also behind the jailbreak and the deaths of Willett's lawmen. If that was the case, then Clint also knew to be on the lookout for those men as well when he got to that cabin near the mountains.

There was only two ways for him to find out for sure what this was all about and how it was going to end. Clint could either sit back and wait for it to happen, or he could charge into the fray, forcing the players to show their hands.

Just as in a tense game of poker, everything boiled down to matching one hand against another. After all the bluffing, betting, cheating and second-guessing, that's all it ever came down to.

One hand against another.

Win or lose.

The town faded behind Clint and Eclipse amid the thundering of hooves. In fact, no matter how dangerous it was for himself, Clint felt better once Willett and all its residents were left in the dust. That just left him, the killers and whatever ambush they had planned.

Of course, Clint didn't figure on riding straight down the path Rackton had marked on his map. That would make things a little too easy. It had been a while since Clint had traveled through those parts, but he didn't have to be intimately familiar with the place to know that there was more than one way to that cabin.

Already, Clint was searching the trail ahead of him for any alternate paths that might serve his purposes. He was about a mile away from the fork marked on Rackton's map when he caught a glimpse of something that might just suit his needs. It wasn't much more than a row of trees that sat a bit higher than the rest, but it told Clint that there was probably something bringing those trees up above the others.

And where there was an elevated section of land, there could very well be a narrow trail leading up toward the mountains. By the looks of it, the trail ran alongside the one Clint was currently on, which made it look all the better. Even if there was no trail, a ridge looking down on the area was just what he needed.

There was less than a mile to go before he reached the fork on the map. Clint slowed Eclipse to a quick walk and started looking for a spot that caught his attention.

He saw it less than a minute later and pulled back on his reins.

The trees lining the path thinned out slightly, allowing Clint to see a little ways through to what was on the other side. Sure enough, there was a ridge there which led up along a wooded slope. Not wanting to waste any more time or allow himself to get any closer to the proposed meeting spot, Clint swung down from the saddle and led Eclipse off the trail to an area hidden from the casual eye.

"All right, boy," he said while tying the stallion to one of the trees. "Wait here and I'll head off on my own. My guess is that Rackton is expecting me to come as fast as I can, so they're probably already waiting for me."

Speaking quietly to organize his thoughts, Clint planned what he was going to do, while making one last check to prepare himself. He filled the loops on his gun belt with extra ammunition for the Colt and then removed the rifle from its holster on Eclipse's side. All the while, he kept his senses alert for any hint that someone had found him. But as far as he could tell, he and the Darley Arabian were the only two souls in the immediate vicinity.

Up until this point, Clint had been using his anger and frustration with what had happened to speed him along his way. He knew that such emotions wouldn't do him any good in a fight, so he took a moment to pull in a few calming breaths and get himself focused on the task at hand.

Letting Rackton get him angry would only be playing into the killer's hands. Such tactics were crude, but extremely effective, and it took a good amount of self-control for Clint to put aside the memories of those dead lawmen and the tears in Anne's eyes.

Once his mind was calm and focused, Clint turned toward the ridge and started heading to it. His eyes scanned the ground for anything that might make a sound, which his feet were quick to avoid. His ears fixed on anything that might give away the presence of an enemy, and his trigger finger was ready for however many targets Rackton had lined up against him.

FORTY-THREE

The cabin was empty. All three men that had been waiting inside its leaning walls were scattered throughout the surrounding terrain. The guns that had been collected on the table were no longer there, having been distributed to all four men bound by the blood that they had already and were about to spill.

It was too late for any of them to turn back now. The three bank robbers knew that well enough. As much as they hated to admit it, they knew Rackton was right. Looking over your shoulder was no way to spend your life . . . especially when you were in the sights of someone like Clint Adams.

Mark Rackton had no intention of turning back. On the contrary, he was a man in his glory, if not his element. His fancy clothes were pulled tightly around him like the smooth black shell of a beetle. He slithered from spot to spot, keeping as much to the shadows as possible, ducking out of the moonlight as though it burned his pale skin.

He looked up at the sky, which he could barely see through the canopy of trees that hung over his head. Stars winked back at him like knowing conspirators as he lifted one pistol in hand and pressed its ivory handle against his cheek. The gun felt cool and comforting. The air brushed against his skin.

Everything was right with the world.

His time, Rackton knew, had come.

Just as those warm thoughts pulsed through his mind, he heard the snap of branches beneath someone's foot. Rackton peered around his tree at the spot where the noise had come from. All night long, Ben and his partners had been tramping about in the darkness like a bunch of club-footed monkeys. At the very least, he knew they were going to fulfill their function perfectly.

Rackton stood in the darkness without making a move. His thumb tensed on the pistol's hammer as he waited for the source of the noise to show itself. Sure enough, it was Henry, who'd moved from his post. The robber was supposed to be in one of the sniper nests that Rackton had scouted out, but was instead walking around as if without a care in the world.

That didn't matter, though. In fact, Rackton was surprised Henry had stayed put as long as he had and was glad to see him walking about. After all, how was the moron supposed to draw Adams's fire if he stayed put?

Anders had been laying flat on his stomach for what felt like an eternity. There were rocks digging into his knees and twigs poking him at all angles. The spot he'd been shown seemed secluded enough, but there still seemed to be plenty of ways for someone to sneak up on him.

Perhaps it was his discomfort, or the hours of boredom, but the robber would have much rather been still walking around the perimeter of that old cabin than planting himself like a weed in the cold night air.

He sighted down the barrel of his rifle and checked to make sure it was loaded, just as he had countless times before. With nothing moving around him and all the others hidden away in their own spots, there was precious little else to fill the man's time.

Suddenly, he heard a twig snapping behind him. Anders held his breath and his heart skipped a beat. Ben and Rackton had told him that Adams should be headed along this trail, which was why he'd been posted in a spot overlooking it. But now that he actually heard someone coming, he started to feel like a sheet that had been hung out to dry on a laundry line.

His mind raced with all the little details that Rackton had told him about where to lead Adams if he was chased and where he could hide if he needed to. Sweat formed on his palms and started to itch as it soaked into the wooden rifle stock.

He waited and strained his ears to catch another snapping twig, but only caught the restless churning of the wind. When he was just about to let out the breath he'd been holding, Anders heard the subtle rustle of something moving against the ground. At that moment, he pinpointed the spot where it had come from.

Behind him.

The sound had come from behind him, just like the snapping twig before it.

Filled with a sense of panic that stabbed at his innards like a hot branding iron, Anders rolled onto his back and twisted around to look behind him. He swung the rifle around and worked the lever, wondering what could have come down from the mountainside without him hearing it until that very instant.

The first thing he saw was the mountain range stretching up over him like the broad chest of a giant. Pressing the rifle against his shoulder, Anders glared through its sights while desperately trying to find a target.

Instead, there was nothing. Not one trace of movement. Not even another sound for him to focus on. All he could see was the swaying shapes of the trees and the dark form of the mountain looming over his position.

It took a bit of concentration, but Anders finally was able to listen to something besides the rush of blood through his own veins and the thumping in his chest.

"Jesus Christ," he whispered. "There's nothin' there."

Relieved by his own words, Anders rolled back onto his stomach to look back down at the trail. But instead of the familiar stretch of road that he'd been watching, he saw a solid black shape obscuring everything else.

His heart leapt up into his throat and his hands reflexively brought the rifle up to bear on whatever was standing in front of him. But the weapon wouldn't move from the ground no matter how much he struggled to lift it. The rifle seemed to be stuck to the dirt, and a dull, crushing pain flooded through his hand.

Looking up, Anders got a close look at the boot that was pressing down on his fingers, holding the rifle against the ground. Anders strained his neck as his other hand went for the pistol at his side. His fingers had touched his second weapon's handle when his eyes finally locked upon the face staring down at him.

Clint Adams studied Anders for less than a second. As he stooped down, Clint's foot pressed even harder against Anders's hand, causing the robber to grit his teeth and grunt with pain.

That grunt was all Anders could get out before a blinding pain in the back of his head caused his teeth to rattle inside his skull. His instincts pressed him to draw his pistol and use it, but his body was unable to comply. The edges of his vision were getting fuzzy and all his strength was leaking out.

Finally, after letting out a haggard breath, Anders dropped his face to the ground and all his muscles went limp.

Clint crouched over the other man, lifting his arms up

in preparation for another strike. Even in the dim moon-light, he could see the robber's eyes glaze over and his head loll to one side. Knowing that another blow to the head wouldn't be necessary, Clint let his own rifle drop to his side and scooped up the one belonging to Anders.

Taking position next to the robber, Clint lowered him-self down onto his belly so that he would be out of sight. His eyes searched the surrounding area for a hint as to where the next target would be. Finding this one had been easy enough, especially while moving along the narrow ridge above the trail.

All Clint had had to do was look down and see the robber laying on the ground below. A little quiet maneu-vering and a few distracting noises had sealed the deal, giving Clint all the advantage he'd needed to take out one of his potential bushwhackers.

Rather than get excited about his victory, Clint emptied the shells from Anders's rifle and tossed them into the bushes. He moved on after tying Anders up like a hog at a county fair, leaving the robber to sleep where he'd landed.

FORTY-FOUR

One of the shadows didn't stay where it belonged.

By the time he heard the scuffle where Anders was positioned, Rackton was perfectly comfortable moving around in the darkness. His eyes were adjusted to the gloom and his feet knew right where to step so that he would blend seamlessly into the night.

Even so, he was taken a little by surprise when he accidentally spotted Clint moving in closer to the cabin. Rackton had been looking at one spot and turned to look at another. When his eyes drifted back to their original position, he saw that one of the shadows that had been there before was missing.

He froze in his spot and looked harder, going over every detail and comparing it to the mental picture he'd built up over the last several days. Only then did he see the other figure moving stealthily behind the bushes. Rackton smiled and nodded with satisfaction.

Clint Adams was proving to be a worthy opponent, indeed. In fact, he'd already gotten around a few of the traps that Rackton had set. The gunman sunk back into the shadows and headed toward one of the many lethal spots he'd failed to mention to anyone else. Along the way, he kept an eye on where Clint Adams was moving. He could see the Gunsmith now that he knew exactly where to look.

Henry and Ben, on the other hand, didn't seem to be so lucky.

"I thought I told you to stay put," Ben hissed when he saw Henry walking toward him.

The other robber moved up right beside the fat man and hunkered down. "I heard something further up the trail," Henry replied, completely ignoring the first statement. "Maybe we should both check it out."

Ben was about to respond when he snapped his hand up and looked around nervously. His large, oddly shaped body was not built for blending into the shadows and he felt about as comfortable as a cat in a bathtub.

Without saying a word, the fat man pointed toward the north and thumbed back the hammer of his pistol.

Henry looked right where Ben was pointing. He couldn't do much more than that, however, before a dark shape came rushing toward him. Taking a shot out of gut reflex, Henry pulled his trigger even though he couldn't make out anything but a dark shape against a dark background. Knowing that bullet would go wild, Henry was already preparing to fire again when he started making out some details of what was coming at him.

There was a shape roughly the size of a man and there was also something long and narrow flying directly toward him.

That last detail caused Henry to stop short and raise his hands up reflexively in front of him. The rifle came sailing through the air to knock against Henry's forearms. There wasn't much power behind it, but as soon as Henry dropped his arms, Clint was practically on top of him.

Clint sent a quick jab into Henry's stomach using the butt of his rifle. The robber was tensed for it and absorbed most of the impact with a slight grunt. Feeling his blood pump through him in a rush, Henry could think of nothing else except for saving his own life and snuffing out the life within the man in front of him.

For a man weighed down by restricting bulk, Ben moved surprisingly quick. He saw Clint move toward Henry, but didn't have a clear shot without possibly putting a bullet through his own partner. Rather than wait for an opening to present itself, the fat man waddled away toward one of the hiding spots Rackton had pointed out to him.

Locked in close combat, Henry didn't see Ben leave and wasn't even concerned about the other man. All he saw was Clint trying to take another swing at him using the rifle as a club. Henry ducked under Clint's swing and sent an uppercut straight into his midsection.

As soon as he'd missed with the rifle, Clint prepared himself for a follow-up blow from the robber. He wasn't disappointed and quickly felt Henry's fist slam against his solar plexus. Even though he'd tensed himself for the punch, Clint still felt his breath melt out of his lungs and dull pain course along his nerves.

Henry straightened up so that he was looking Clint square in the eye. Without wasting another second, he lifted his pistol and started squeezing the trigger.

Seeing the flash of moonlight against gunmetal, Clint let his rifle drop and stepped back with his left foot. As he moved into a classic duelist's position, Clint plucked the Colt from its holster with a hand that flickered like lightning from one spot to another.

Henry dropped the hammer of his pistol and sent a bullet exploding from his barrel. The chunk of lead burned into the air, driving straight through the spot where Clint's heart had been before he'd moved. Now, the round caught mostly empty space, ripping a shallow trench through Clint's shirt and the front of his chest.

The bullet ripped across his flesh like an animal's claw and sent a sharp pain through Clint's body. That, combined with the motion of his body, was enough to pull Clint's aim slightly off target.

So, when his Colt went off, it drilled a hole through Henry's right eye instead of the middle of his skull. That bought Henry an additional second of life, making it possible for him to feel his back hit the ground before oblivion came rushing in to claim him.

Clint looked around for the last of the robbers and could only find darkness. Although the shadows were thick, there wasn't one of them big enough to hide the fat man that had been there only seconds before. As he was wondering how someone like that could have slipped away so easily, Clint stopped and forced himself to keep still.

Every instinct inside of him was screaming for him to move; his ears were already burning with the gunshot he was expecting to hear at any second. But despite all of that, he held his ground and waited.

FORTY-FIVE

Ben kept his back pressed up against cold, unyielding rock. He used his left hand to hold up a thin wall of branches which had been lashed together with twine to form something similar to a crude hunter's blind. Rackton has showed him where that blind had been stashed, and Ben had gone to it the moment he saw Clint Adams take on Henry.

The branches were entwined and spaced just far enough apart for Ben's fingers to slip between them. There were just enough leaves on the twigs to hide the fat man from anyone who didn't know exactly what to look for.

In daylight, the blind would have stood out. In darkness, however, it was more than enough to shield him for the moment.

Slowly, being careful not to scrape his hand against the back of the twigs, Ben lifted his gun with his free hand and started easing its barrel through the leaves. He could just make out the shape of Clint Adams standing over Henry's body.

All he had to do was stay right there for another couple of seconds . . .

• • •

Clint knew damn well that Ben couldn't have gotten far. No matter how quick or agile a man could be, there was no physical way for someone of Ben's size to sneak away amid all these bushes. The ground might have been rocky and solid closer to the trail, but not where they were at the moment.

If Ben was moving, Clint would have heard it. And since he couldn't hear anything, Clint knew that the other man was standing still somewhere real close. And since he couldn't see him, that meant Ben had found somewhere to hide. That wasn't surprising since this whole area had been scouted out for an ambush in the first place.

So far, Clint had survived by doing things that the other men hadn't expected. In this particular situation, knowing that he was being targeted at that very second, the last thing Clint should have been doing was standing still in the same spot that Ben had left him.

On the other hand, if he hadn't been standing still and keeping quiet, Clint might not have spotted the large, oddly shaped bush less than twenty feet away. And if he hadn't been keeping absolutely quiet, he might not have heard the faint *click* of a hammer being snapped back into firing position.

Relying on gut instinct even more than what little his senses could make out, Clint shifted his hips and pivoted so he could take aim on that bush. In the split second between his finger clenching on the trigger and the bullet exploding into the air, Clint's mind swam with the grim possibilities he faced.

Ben could very well get a shot off at any second. Since the fat man was probably taking his time and aiming, he could also very well put that bullet right through Clint's heart or head.

While unexpected, holding his ground could very well have been the worst—not to mention last—mistake of Clint's life.

All of that rushed through him in a flash that showed only as a twinge in Clint's right eye. Just as he'd expected, Ben did manage to pull his trigger, but not until Clint's bullet had punched through the blind and lodged deeply into his chest.

Clint didn't wait to see if he'd hit his target. Instead, he fired again and again, riddling the spot with bullets until finally the blind dropped away to reveal the man it had been hiding.

Still clenching his gun, Ben staggered forward to follow up his first, wild shot. Every one of Clint's bullets had struck him, but none had gotten through his bulk to hit anything vital enough to put him down. Ben sucked in another breath, lifted his gun . . .

Now that he had something to sight on, Clint adjusted his aim and sent the last of his Colt's rounds into Ben's face.

The fat man took another half-step forward, dropped to his knees, and fell face-first to the ground. His gun went off one last time, sending its round into the earth.

Clint immediately started plucking rounds from his gun belt. He knew that Rackton was around here somewhere and didn't plan on giving the bastard a free shot at him before he could reload. Of course, not all plans work out so well.

"Toss the pistol, Adams," came a sneering voice from behind Clint.

Before Clint could respond, he felt the touch of steel against the back of his skull, quickly followed by the snap of a hammer.

"Toss it or die."

Fresh out of options, Clint tossed the Colt.

FORTY-SIX

Rackton smiled, but didn't allow himself to get any closer to Clint than was necessary. "Finally," he said. "I've got my day in the sun."

The pistol dragged along the back of Clint's head as Rackton walked around to stand in front of him. Once he could see the other man, Clint stared into his eyes and said, "You call this your moment in the sun? Your big victory?"

"I'd say it could be considered a victory. After all, you're unarmed and I'm one second away from hollowing out that skull of yours. I've been waiting for this for years."

Clint shook his head. "I remember you now. I let you go because you didn't seem worth any more of my time. Did you think I was coming after you? Is that why you went through all of this?"

"I went through all of this to get back what you took from me."

"What's that? Your pride?"

Nodding, Rackton said, "Yes. My pride. My dignity. But there was something more than that. Do you know how many robberies I've pulled off, Adams?"

"No. But I'm guessing you'll tell me."

"Ninety-nine. Those started from my first when I was ten and go up to the last a couple years ago. I stole enough money to make me rich a dozen times over, but I found that I didn't have any interest in going for job number one hundred.

"I could have, you know. They were all so easy. And that's where you come in. When I met you in New Mexico, you ran me out of town like I was nothing. I wanted to kill you more than life itself. But when that wore off, I still wanted to go after you because you presented me with something that truly inspired me. You were a *challenge,* Mr. Adams. Finding you, trapping you, killing you—it was all a challenge that nobody else has been man enough to meet. But I have."

Clint slowly dug the toe of his boot into the dirt, keeping his eyes locked on Rackton's. "It doesn't take much of a man to jump out from hiding to bushwhack someone. You want a challenge? Then let's finish this man-to-man."

That wry grin broadened across Rackton's face. "Not interested. I'm not stupid, Adams. And I'm not fast enough to beat you in a fair fight. Executing you suits me just fine. In fact, you should take this as a compliment."

Still inching his boot farther along the ground, Clint moved slow enough so that the leather didn't scrape noisily across steel. "So you broke these guys out of jail to use them as bait?"

"Yeah," Rackton answered plainly. "And they were just desperate enough to play their part without too many questions." Rackton's eyes hardened into a cold, lethal stare as his finger began tightening around the trigger. "You've got to admit, Adams. This whole thing came together rather impressively."

"Impressive?" Clint asked as he snapped his foot upward.

The boot that he'd been sliding forward was all the way

under the rifle that he'd dropped when facing Henry. As
he lifted that foot up, it sent the rifle leaping off the
ground just high enough for him to pluck it out of the air.
In one fluid motion, he spun the rifle in a tight, vertical
circle which caught Rackton's gun hand right on the
knuckles.

Pain shot through Rackton's hand, but he didn't drop
the pistol. As he desperately tried to bring it to bear again
on his intended, Clint worked the lever and the rifle
barked once, blasting a hole through Rackton's chest.

Clint took a moment to savor the turn of events. "Now
that," he said, "was impressive."

Watch for

TREASURE HUNT

255th novel in the exciting GUNSMITH series
from Jove

Coming in March!